Witchcraft Classics
Best Witch Short Stories
1800-1849

**Edited
by
Andrew Barger**

AndrewBarger.com

To my father, Gary Lee Barger.

Fiction
Coffee with Poe: A Novel of Edgar Allan Poe's Life
The Divine Dantes: Squirt Guns in Hades (Book I)
The Divine Dantes: Paella in Purgatory (Book II)
The Divine Dantes: Cruising in Paradise (Book III)
Mailboxes – Mansions – Memphistopheles

Anthologies Edited

1800-1849
Shifters: Best Werewolf Short Stories 1800-1849
Middle Unearthed: Best Fantasy Short Stories 1800-1849
BlooDeath: Best Vampire Stories 1800-1849
Mesaerion: Best Science Fiction Stories 1800-1849
Phantasmal: Best Ghost Stories 1800-1849
6a66le: Best Horror Short Stories 1800-1849
Orion: An Epic English Poem

1850-1899
Fright: Best Horror Short Stories 1850-1899
Specters: Best Ghost Short Stories 1850-1899
Leo Tolstoy's 20 Greatest Short Stories Annotated
Leo Tolstoy's 5 Greatest Novellas Annotated

Contents

Hags! Hags! Hags!

WITCH STORIES! AS the ancient saying goes, let's start at the beginning. There were three watershed moments for witch stories before the 19th century. First, in the late 8th or early 7th century B.C. Homer wrote *The Odyssey* and with it introduced the world to one of the first witches. He named her Circe. In book 12, Circe uses a concoction of herbs to turn Odysseus's men into swine.

Fast forward three hundred years, circa 550 B.C., and one of the most popular stories of a hag was published in the Bible, of all places. The Biblical Witch of Endor, found in I Samuel 28:3-25 brought conjuring of the dead to the forefront of bewitching powers. In the story, Saul visits a witch to consult with the deceased Samuel about a forthcoming battle with the Philistines. Saul wants to know the outcome and God has forsaken him. The Witch of Endor summons the former king of Israel and he tells Saul that his army will be defeated, and that tomorrow his relatives will join Samuel in the afterlife. Before the book of Samuel is the book of Exodus. In Exodus 22:18 (Geneva and King James translations) we find the interesting statement, "Thou Shalt Not Suffer a Witch to Live . . .."

Although people were apparently instructed to persecute witches in the Geneva translation of the Bible used by the Puritans who conducted the Salem witch trials, and throughout Europe for centuries, one must advance more than a thousand years before witches once again play centerstage in popular literature. Enter William Shakespeare and 1623 when he gave the world his famous three hags of *Macbeth* (4.1.47-60):

MACBETH
"How now, you secret, black and midnight, hags!
"What is't you do?"

WITCHES
"A deed without a name."

Like the Witch of Endor, the tri-hags of *Macbeth* are enabled with the power to conjure spirits. It is no coincidence that later in the same century, the infamous Salem, Massachusetts witch trials took place in America. A man by the name of John Hathorne served as a judge at the trials. He also turned out to be the great-great grandfather of Nathaniel Hawthorne (born with the surname Hathorne), author of two of the best witch short stories in this anthology for the 50 year period from 1800-1849. It is this period when these stories took flight, but not on broomsticks despite the record of accused witches at the Salem Witch Trials that they "ride upon stickes . . .."

Below is Judge Hathorne's line of questioning directed at Sarah Osburne, an accused witch in 1690, who tormented children in the village. The text was compiled by William Elliot Woodward in the *Records of Salem Witchcraft*.[1] (Note that in Old English v was used for u.)

"Mr Hathorn desired all the children to stand up and look upon her and see if they did know her, which they all did and every one of them said that this was one of the women that did afflict them, and that they had constantly seen her in the very habit, that shee was now in, theire evidence do stand that shee said this morning that shee was more like to be bewitched, than that shee was a witch. Mr Hathorn asked her what made her say so, shee answered that shee was frighted one time in her sleep and either saw or dreamed that shee saw a thing like an indian all black which did prick her in her neck and pulled her by the back part of her head to the dore of the house

(H) did you never see anything else.

(0) no. it was said by some in the meeting house that shee had said that shee would never be tied to that lying spirit any more.

(H) what lying spirit is this, hath the devil ever deceived you and been false to you.

(0) I doe not know the devil I never did see him.

(H) what lying spirit was it then.

(0) it was a voice that I thought I heard.

(H) what did it propound to you.

(0) that I should goe no more to meeting, but I said I would and did goe the next Sabbath day.

(H) were you never tempted furder.

---

[1] *Records of Salem Witchcraft*, I (Roxbury, Massachusetts, 1864), 13–48.

(0) no.

(H) why did you yield thus far to the devil as never to goe to meeting since

(0) Alas. I have been sike and not able to goe. her husband and others said that shee had not been at meeting this yeare and two months. . . . Salem Village March 1st 1691.

Titiba, an Indian woman brought before vs by Const Joseph Herrick of Salem vpon Suspition of witchcraft by her committed according to ye complaint of Jos. Hutcheson and Thomas Putnam &c of Salem Village as appears p warrant granted Salem 29 ffebry 169½. Titiba vpon examination and after some deny all acknowledged ye matter of fact according to her examination giuen in more fully will appeare, and who also charged Sarah Good and Sarah Osburne with ye same . . .

(H) Titibe whan evil spirit have you familiarity with.

(T) none.

(H) why do you hurt these children.

(T) I do not hurt them,

(H) who is it then.

(T) the devil for ought I know.

(H) Did you never see the devil.

(T) The devil came to me and bid me serve him.

(H) Who have you seen.

(T) Four women sometimes hurt the children.

(H) Who were they.

(T) Goode Osburn and Sarah Good and I doe not know who the other were. Sarah Good and Osburne would have me hurt the children but I would not she further saith there was a tale man of Boston that she did see.

(H) when did you see them.

(T) Last night at Boston.

(H) what did they say to you.

(T) they said hurt the children

(H) and did you hurt them

(T) no there is 4 women and one man they hurt the children and they lay all upon me and they tell me if I will not hurt the children they will hurt me.

(H) but did you not hurt them

(T) yes, but I will hurt them no more.

(H) are you not sorry you did hurt them.

(T) yes.

(H) and why then doe you hurt them.

(T) they say hurt children or wee will doe worse to you.

(H) what have you seen.
(T) an man come to me and say serve me.
(H) what service.
(T) hurt the children and last night there was an appearance that said kill the children and if I would no go on hurting the children they would do worse to me.
(H) what is this appearance you see.
(T) Sometimes it is like a hog and sometimes like a great dog, this appearance shee saith shee did see 4 times.
(H) what did it say to you
(T) it s the black dog said serve me but I said I am afraid he said if I did not he would doe worse to me.
(H) what did you say to it.
(T) I will serve you no longer. then he said he would hurt me and then he looked like a man and threatens to hurt me, shee said that this man had a yellow bird that kept with him and he told me he had more pretty things that he would give me if I would serve him.
(H) what were these pretty things.
(T) he did not show me them.
(H) what also have you seen
(T) two rats, a red rat and a black rat.
(H) what did they say to you.
(T) they said serve me.
(H) when did you see them.
(T) last night and they said serve me, but I said I would not (H) what service.
(T) shee said hurt the children.
(H) did you not pinch Elizabeth Hubbard this morning
(T) the man brought her to me and made me pinch her
(H) why did you goe to Thomas Putnams last night and hurt his child.
(T) they pull and hall me and make me goe
(H) and what would have you doe.
(T) Kill her with a knif.
Left. Fuller and others said at this time when the child saw these persons and was tormented by them that she did complayn of a knife, that they would have her cut her head off with a knife.
(H) how did you go
(T) we ride upon stickes and are there presently.
(H) doe you goe through the trees or over them.
(T) we see nothing but are there presently.
(H) why did you not tell your master.

(T) I was afraid they said they would cut of my head if I told.

(H) would you not have hurt others if you cold.

(T) They said they would hurt others but they could not

(H) what attendants hath Sarah Good.

(T) a yellow bird and shee would have given me one

(H) what meate did she give it

(T) it did suck her between her fingers.

(H) did not you hurt Mr Currins child

(T) Goode Good and Goode Osburn told that they did hurt Mr Currens child and would have had me hurt him two, but I did not.

(H) what hath Sarah Osburn.

(T) yellow dog, shee had a thing with a head like a woman with 2 legges, and wings. Abigail Williams that lives with her Uncle Parris said that she did see the same creature, and it turned into the shape of Goode Osburn.

(H) what else have you seen with Osburn.

(T) another thing, hairy it goes upright like a man it hath only 2 leggs.

(H) did you not see Sarah Good upon Elizabeth Hubbard, last Saterday.

(T) I did see her set a wolfe upon her to afflict her, the with this maid did say that she did complain of a wolfe.

(H) what persons

(T) shee further saith that shee saw a cat with Good at another time.

(H) What cloathes doth the man go in

(T) he goes in black clouthes a tal man with white hair I thinke

(H)] How doth the woman go

(T) in a white whood and a black whood with a top knot

(H) doe you see who it is that torments these children now.

(T) yes it is Goode Good, shee hurts them in her own shape

(H) and who is it that hurts them now.

(T) I cannot see. I am blind now.

Salem Village

March the 1st 1691

Written by Ezekiell Cheevers.

Salem Village March 1 1691"

But enough about the Salem Witch Trials. Combing old magazines, newspapers, journals and scholarly articles, I uncovered twenty-five witch stories originally written in the English language over one hundred years after the horrific events in Salem. The witch trials had a lasting effect in both the U.S. and Europe, with the majority published in European magazines.

The authors in this important time period for witch stories believed strongly in the ability of witches to shapeshift into small four-legged animals such as cats and hares. Above all, each witch is called a "hag" (or "hagg") or a "withered crone" or a "creature" or an "old spinster;" in sum, a single elderly woman, never married, who holds a grudge against society and sets about in her little cave or hovel to exact revenge on a world that has cruelly turned its back on her. This is how William Darby describes them in "Lydia Ashbaugh." "When a woman is single, old, ugly, and of all things else, *poor*, she is a witch . . .." There are no beautiful, young witches practicing their incantations that became popular in the following century. No. The witches of 1800-1849 are all hags with no exceptions.

Hags! Hags! Hags!

But what about the authors of these classic witch stories? They are certainly no hags. From whither do they hail? By happenstance, authors from many different countries are presented in this anthology. There are four countries represented by the authors of the seven witch stories in this collection. The United States produced four of the stories, with two being by Nathaniel Hawthorne. Ireland, Russia and Scotland are each represented by a single author. It is surprising that none of the authors are from England and while the Brothers Grimm wrote "The Old Witch" and published it in Germany during 1812, it does not rise to the level of this collection.

Hawthorne's "Young Goodman Brown" is the most popular in this collection and is worth revisiting if you have read it before. I believe, however, "The Hollow of the Three Hills" is Hawthorne's best witch story. It was published in the *Salem Gazette* on November 12, 1830, and likely influenced by Sir Walter Scott's publication of his *Letters on Demonology and Witchcraft* on September 14, 1830, which served as a popular account of the supernatural in letter-form to his son-in-law. Hawthorne certainly had an affinity for witches. Besides the two short stories collected here,

Hawthorne included a witch named Ann Hibbins[2] in *The Scarlet Letter*. Next there is Samuel Lover's "The Marvelous Legend of Tom Connor's Cat." This humorous witch story will leave you guessing until the end. Lover's tale is followed with one by Elizabeth Ellet, the only female author that wrote one of the best witch stories for this period.

Her tale, "The Witch Caprusche," is quite good, though its genesis is not of Ellet's original creation. James Hogg penned two witch short stories with "The Brownie of the Black Haggs" being his best. A decade later, he published "The Witches of Traquair," which is full of biting humor. Both stories pale in the face of William Darby's pseudonymously tale "Lydia Ashbaugh, the Witch" in January 1836. Yet, there was no reason to hide his name given that "Lydia Ashbaugh," in my view, is America's first *great* witch story. Witches again took center stage. Last in this collection appears Nikolai Gogol. He is the only Russian author to make an appearance. He gave the world many excellent short stories and "Viy" is one of his best. I hope you enjoy every creepy word of it.

As with the other supernatural anthologies, included are background information for each author and story. At the end of the anthology is a list of witch short stories considered.

With Love and Witchcraft,

Andrew Barger

---

[2] Ann Hibbins was a real woman reported to have lived in the Massachusetts Bay Colony where the Salem witch trials took place. Hibbins was executed to death as a witch in 1656.

Nathaniel Hawthorne
(1804-1864)

Introduction
"The Hollow of the Three Hills"

It is little realized that "Young Goodman Brown," which Nathaniel Hawthorne published in 1835, was not his first witch story. "The Hollow of the Three Hills" was published half a decade earlier, *Salem Gazette* on November 12, 1830. It is a better story in both context and writing than the former. The shadowy witch story, perhaps most importantly, is not slowed by pervasive symbolism or underlying meaning.

In April 1842, Edgar Allan Poe called it "[a]mong his best. . .." in his "Review of *Twice-Told Tales*," published in *Graham's Magazine*. The following month, in a more fleshed out review in *Graham's*, Poe confessed that he thought the witch theme of showing the future and the past was well-trodden, yet liked the story "as affording an excellent example of the author's peculiar ability. The subject is common-place. A witch subjects the Distant and the Past to the view of a mourner. It has been the fashion to describe, in such cases, a mirror in which the images of the absent appear; or a cloud of smoke is made to arise, and thence the figures are gradually unfolded. Mr. Hawthorne has wonderfully heightened his effect by making the ear, in place of the eye, the medium by which the fantasy is conveyed. The head of the mourner is enveloped in the cloak of the witch, and within its magic folds there arise sounds which have an all-sufficient intelligence. Throughout this article also, the artist is conspicuous — not more in positive than in negative merits. Not only is all done that should be done, but (what perhaps is an end with more difficulty attained) there is nothing done which should not be. Every word *tells*, and there is not a word which does *not* tell."

As Poe recognized, witches are seers and they are often consulted by those with a desire to *know*, undoubtedly with terrible results.

The Hollow of the Three Hills
1830

IN THOSE STRANGE old times, when fantastic dreams and madmen's reveries were realized among the actual circumstances of life, two persons met together at an appointed hour and place. One was a lady, graceful in form and fair of feature, though pale and troubled, and smitten with an untimely blight in what should have been the fullest bloom of her years; the other was an ancient and meanly-dressed woman, of ill-favored aspect, and so withered, shrunken, and decrepit, that even the space since she began to decay must have exceeded the ordinary term of human existence.

In the spot where they encountered, no mortal could observe them. Three little hills stood near each other, and down in the midst of them sunk a hollow basin, almost mathematically circular, two or three hundred feet in breadth, and of such depth that a stately cedar might but just be visible above the sides. Dwarf pines were numerous upon the hills, and partly fringed the outer verge of the intermediate hollow, within which there was nothing but the brown grass of October, and here and there a tree trunk that had fallen long ago, and lay mouldering with no green successsor from its roots. One of these masses of decaying wood, formerly a majestic oak, rested close beside a pool of green and sluggish water at the bottom of the basin. Such scenes as this (so gray tradition tells) were once the resort of the Power of Evil and his plighted subjects; and here, at midnight or on the dim verge of evening, they were said to stand round the mantling pool, disturbing its putrid waters in the performance of an impious baptismal rite. The chill beauty of an autumnal sunset was now gilding the three hill-tops, whence a paler tint stole down their sides into the hollow.

"Here is our pleasant meeting come to pass," said the aged crone, "according as thou hast desired. Say quickly what thou wouldst have of me, for there is but a short hour that we may tarry here."

As the old withered woman spoke, a smile glimmered on her countenance, like lamplight on the wall of a sepulchre. The lady trembled, and cast her eyes upward to the verge of the basin, as if meditating to return with her purpose unaccomplished. But it was not so ordained.

"I am a stranger in this land, as you know," said she at length. "Whence I come it matters not; but I have left those behind me with whom my fate was intimately bound, and from whom I am cut off forever. There is a weight in my bosom that I cannot away with, and I have come hither to inquire of their welfare."

"And who is there by this green pool that can bring thee news from the ends of the earth?" cried the old woman, peering into the lady's face. "Not from my lips mayst thou hear these tidings; yet, be thou bold, and the daylight shall not pass away from yonder hill-top before thy wish be granted."

"I will do your bidding though I die," replied the lady desperately.

The old woman seated herself on the trunk of the fallen tree, threw aside the hood that shrouded her gray locks, and beckoned her companion to draw near.

"Kneel down," she said, "and lay your forehead on my knees."

She hesitated a moment, but the anxiety that had long been kindling burned fiercely up within her. As she knelt down, the border of her garment was dipped into the pool; she laid her forehead on the old woman's knees, and the latter drew a cloak about the lady's face, so that she was in darkness. Then she heard the muttered words of prayer, in the midst of which she started, and would have arisen.

"Let me flee,–let me flee and hide myself, that they may not look upon me!" she cried. But, with returning recollection, she hushed herself, and was still as death.

For it seemed as if other voices–familiar in infancy, and unforgotten through many wanderings, and in all the vicissitudes of her heart and fortune--were mingling with the accents of the prayer. At first the words were faint and indistinct, not rendered so by distance, but rather resembling the dim pages of a book which we strive to read by an imperfect and gradually brightening light. In such a manner, as the prayer proceeded, did those voices strengthen upon the ear; till at length the petition ended, and the conversation of an aged man, and of a woman broken and decayed like himself, became distinctly audible to the lady as she knelt. But those strangers appeared not to stand in the hollow depth between the three hills. Their voices were encompassed and reechoed by the walls of a chamber, the windows of which were rattling in the breeze; the regular vibration of a clock, the crackling of a fire, and the tinkling of the embers as they fell among the ashes, rendered the scene almost as vivid as if painted to the eye. By a melancholy hearth sat these two old people, the man calmly despondent, the woman querulous and tearful, and their words were all of sorrow. They spoke of a daughter, a wanderer they knew not where, bearing dishonor along with her, and leaving shame and affliction to bring their gray heads to the grave. They alluded also to other and more recent woe, but in the midst of their talk their voices seemed to melt into the sound of the wind sweeping mournfully among the autumn leaves; and when the lady lifted her eyes, there was she kneeling in the hollow between three hills.

"A weary and lonesome time yonder old couple have of it," remarked the old woman, smiling in the lady's face.

"And did you also hear them?" exclaimed she, a sense of intolerable humiliation triumphing over her agony and fear.

"Yea; and we have yet more to hear," replied the old woman. "Wherefore, cover thy face quickly."

Again the withered hag poured forth the monotonous words of a prayer that was not meant to be acceptable in heaven; and soon, in the pauses of her breath, strange murmurings began to thicken, gradually increasing so as to drown and overpower the charm by which they grew. Shrieks pierced through the obscurity of sound, and were succeeded by the singing of sweet female voices, which, in their turn, gave way to a wild roar of laughter, broken suddenly by groanings and sobs, forming altogether a ghastly confusion of terror and mourning and mirth. Chains were rattling, fierce and stern voices uttered threats, and the scourge resounded at their command. All these noises deepened and became substantial to the listener's ear, till she could distinguish every soft and dreamy accent of the love songs that died causelessly into funeral hymns. She shuddered at the unprovoked wrath which blazed up like the spontaneous kindling of flames and she grew faint at the fearful merriment raging miserably around her. In the midst of this wild scene, where unbound passions jostled each other in a drunken career, there was one solemn voice of a man, and a manly and melodious voice it might once have been. He went to and fro continually, and his feet sounded upon the floor. In each member of that frenzied company, whose own burning thoughts had become their exclusive world, he sought an auditor for the story of his individual wrong, and interpreted their laughter and tears as his reward of scorn or pity. He spoke of woman's perfidy, of a wife who had broken her holiest vows, of a home and heart made desolate. Even as he went on, the shout, the laugh, the shriek the sob, rose up in unison, till they changed into the hollow, fitful, and uneven sound of the wind, as it fought among the pine-trees on those three lonely hills. The lady looked up, and there was the withered woman smiling in her face.

"Couldst thou have thought there were such merry times in a madhouse?" inquired the latter.

"True, true," said the lady to herself; "there is mirth within its walls, but misery, misery without."

"Wouldst thou hear more?" demanded the old woman.

"There is one other voice I would fain listen to again," replied the lady, faintly.

"Then, lay down thy head speedily upon my knees, that thou mayst get thee hence before the hour be past."

The golden skirts of day were yet lingering upon the hills, but deep shades obscured the hollow and the pool, as if sombre night were rising thence to overspread the world. Again that evil woman began to weave her spell. Long did it proceed unanswered, till the knolling of a bell stole in among the intervals of her words, like a clang that had travelled far over valley and rising ground, and was just ready to die in the air. The lady shook upon her companion's knees as she heard that boding sound. Stronger it grew and sadder, and deepened into the tone of a death bell, knolling dolefully from some ivy-mantled tower, and bearing tidings of mortality and woe to the cottage, to the hall, and to the solitary wayfarer that all might weep for the doom appointed in turn to them. Then came a measured tread, passing slowly, slowly on, as of mourners with a coffin, their garments trailing on the ground, so that the ear could measure the length of their melancholy array. Before them went the priest, reading the burial service, while the leaves of his book were rustling in the breeze. And though no voice but his was heard to speak aloud, still there were revilings and anathemas, whispered but distinct, from women and from men, breathed against the daughter who had wrung the aged hearts of her parents,–the wife who had betrayed the trusting fondness of her husband,–the mother who had sinned against natural affection, and left her child to die. The sweeping sound of the funeral train faded away like a thin vapor, and the wind, that just before had seemed to shake the coffin pall, moaned sadly round the verge of the Hollow between three Hills. But when the old woman stirred the kneeling lady, she lifted not her head.

"Here has been a sweet hour's sport!" said the withered crone, chuckling to herself.

Samuel Lover
(1797-1868)

Introduction
"The Marvelous Legend of Tom Connor's Cat"

Samuel Lover, born in Dublin, Ireland in 1797, was a self-taught artist of many varieties. He died from bronchitis in 1868. Consider the first paragraph from "The Life of Samuel Lover R.H.A.,"[3] published during 1874 in two volumes: "Poet, novelist, dramatist, painter, etcher, and composer!–it is with this long array of titles, this evidence so rarely met with of a manifold capacity, that we recall the name of Samuel Lover. We cannot look back at the place he occupied for more than a quarter of century without being struck with the fact that, in an age of speciality, he was one of its most notable exceptions. His variety of gift became, practically, the directest challenge to that division of labour principle which forms the law of modern excellence."

It is now apparent the editor should have included "short story author" to the list of many artforms to which Lover was associated. "Handy Andy" is the obvious pseudonym under which "The Marvelous Legend of Tom Connor's Cat"[4] was penned. I have been unable to find any publication that has made this connection. In 1841, Lover published the very popular comedic novel *Handy Andy: A Tale of Irish Life* that saw him reach the height of his popularity. In London he became friends with Charles Dickens and Harrison Ainsworth. The comedic short story in question was published half a decade later in a fantasy book called *Tales of Heroism, and Record of Strange and Wonderful Adventures*. Also published in this influential book is another tale of a witch, "The Unholy Compact Abjured," which does not rise to the level of this anthology.

"The Marvelous Legend of Tom Connor's Cat" is one of the first humorous witch short stories. It stands, in the grand Irish tradition of great storytelling, shoulder to

---

[3] *The Life of Samuel Lover R.H.A.*, Ed. Bayle Bernard, I (London: Henry S. King & Co.) xvii.

[4] Samuel Lover as "Handy Andy," "The Marvelous Legend of Tom Connor's Cat," *Tales of Heroism, and Record of Strange and Wonderful Adventures*, (London: William Mark Clark) 28.

shoulder with Washington Irving's "The Legend of Sleepy Hollow" (1819) and Charles Dickens's "The Goblins Who Stole a Sexton" (1836), as that rare combination of humor and horror that is so difficult to find.

The Marvelous Legend
of
Tom Connor's Cat
1847

"THERE WAS A man in these parts, sir, you must know, called Tom Connor, and he had a cat that was equal to any dozen of rat-traps, and he was proud of the baste, and with rayson; for she was worth her weight in goold to him, in saving his sacks of meal from the thievery of the rats and mice; for Tom was an extensive dealer in corn, and influenced the rise and fall of that article in the market, to the extent of a full dozen of sacks, at a time, which he either kept or sold, as the spirit of free-trade or monopoly came over him. Indeed, at one time, Tom had serious thoughts of applying to the government for a military force to protect his granary, when there was a threatened famine in the county.

"'Pooh! pooh! sir,' said the matter-of-fact little man, 'as if a dozen sacks could be of the smallest consequence in a whole county–pooh! pooh!'

"'Well, sir,' said Murphy, 'I can't help if you don't believe; but it's truth what I am telling you, and pray don't interrupt me, though you may not believe; by the time the story is done you'll have heard more wonderful things than *that*-and besides, remember you're a stranger in these parts, and have no notion of the extraordinary things, physical, metaphysical, and magical, which constitute the idiosyncrasy of rural destiny.'"

"The little man did not know the meaning of Murphy's last sentence–nor Murphy either; but having stopped the little man's throat with the big words, he proceeded.

"This cat, sir, you must know, was a great pet, and was so up to everything, that Tom swore she was a'most like a Christian, only she couldn't speak, and had so sensible look in her eyes, that he was sartain. Sure the chat new every word that was said to her. Well, she used to sit by him at breakfast every morning, and the eloquent cock of her tale, as she used to rub against his leg, said, 'Give me some milk, Tom Connor,' as plain as print, and the plenitude of her purr afterwards, spoke a gratitude beyond language.—Well, one morning, Tom was going to the neighboring town to Market, and he had promised the wife to bring home shoes to the childre', out o' the price of the Corn; and sure enough, before he sat down to breakfast, there was Tom at taking the measure of the childre's feet, by cutting notches on a bit of stick; and the wife gave him so many cautions about getting 'a nate fit' for 'Billy's pretty feet,' that Tom, in his anxiety to nick the closest possible measure, cut off the child's toe. That Disturbed the harmony of the party, and Tom was obliged to breakfast alone, while the mother was endeavoring to cure Billy; in short, trying to make a *heal* of his *toe*. Well, sir, all the time Tom was taking measure for the shoes, the cat was observing him with that luminous peculiarities of I-4 which her tribe is remarkable; and when Tom set down to breakfast, the cat rubbed up against him more vigorously than usual, but time, being bewildered between his expected game and corn, and the positive loss of his child's toe, kept nevermind in her until the cat, with a sort of caterwauling growl, gave Tom a dab of her claws, that went clean through his leather, and a little further.

'Wow,' says Tom with a jump, clapping his hand on the part, and rubbing it, 'By this and that, you drew the blood out o' me,' says Tom, 'you wicked divil–tish,–go along!' says he, making a kick at her. With that the cat gave a reproachful look at him oh, and her eyes glared just like a pair of male-coach lamps in a fog. With that, sir, the cat, with the mysterious '*mi-ow*,' fixed a most penetrating glance on Tom, and distinctly uttered his name.

"Tom felt every hair on his head as stiff as a pump handle–and scarcely crediting his ears, he returned a searching look at the cat, who very quietly proceeded with a sort of nasal twang—

"'Tom Connor,' says she.

"'Yes, ma'am,' says Tom.

"'Come here,' says she, 'whisper–I want to talk to you, Tom,' says she, 'the last taste in private,' says she–rising on her hams, and beckoning him with her paw out o' the door, with a wink and a toss o' the head aiqual to a milliner.

"Well, as you may suppose, Tom didn't know whether he was on his head or heels, but he followed the cat, and off she went and squatted herself under the hedge of a little paddock at the back of Tom's house; and as he came Round the Corner, she held up her paws again, and laid it on her mouth, as much as to say 'be cautious, Tom.' Well, divil a word Tom could say at all, with the fright, so up he goes to the cat, and says she–

"'Tom,' says she, 'I have a great respect for you, and there's something I must tell you, bekase you're losing character with your neighbours,' says she, 'by your goin's on,' says she; 'and it's out o' the respect that I have for you, that I must tell you,' says she.

"'Thank you, ma'am,' says Tom.

"'You're goin off to the town,' says she, 'to buy shoes for the childre',' says she, and never thought o' gettin' me a pair.'

"'You?' says Tom.

"'Yis, me, Tom Connor,' says she; 'and the neighbours wondhers that a respectable man like you, allows your cat to go about the counthry barefutted,' says she.

"'Is it a cat to wear shoes?' says Tom.

"'Why not?' says she, 'doesn't horses wear shoes–and I have a prettier foot than a horse, I hope,' says she, with a toss of her head.

"'Faix, she spakes like a woman; so proud of her feet,' says Tom to himself, astonished, as you may suppose, but pretending never to think it remarkable all the time; and so he went discoursin', and says he, 'it's thrue for you, ma'am,' says he, 'that horses wear shoes-but that stands to rayson, ma'am, you see-seeing the hardship their feet has to go through on the hard roads.'

"'And how do you know what hardship my feet has to go through?' says the cat, mighty sharp.

"'But, ma'am,' says Tom, 'I don't well see how you could fasten a shoe on you,' says he.

"'Lave that to me,' says the cat.

"'Did any one ever stick walnut shells on you, pussey?' says Tom, with a grin.

"'Don't be disrespectful, Tom Connor,' says the cat, with a frown.

"'I ax your pard'n, ma'am,' says he, but as for the horses you wor spakin' about wearin' shoes, you know their shoes is fastened on with nails, and how would your shoes be fastened on?'

"'Ah, you stupid thief,' says she, 'haven't I iligant nails o' my own?' and with that she gave him a dab of her claw, that made him roar.

"'Ow! murdher!' says he.

"'Now, no more of your palaver, Misther Connor,' says the cat, just be off and get me the shoes.'

"'Tare an ouns,' says Tom, what'll become o' me, if I'm to get shoes for my cats?' says he, 'for you increase your family four times a year, and you have six or seven every time, says he, and then you must all have two pair apiece–wirra! wirra!–I'll be ruined in shoe leather,' says Tom.

"'No more o' your stuff,' says the cat, 'don't be standin' here undher the hedge talkin', or we'll lose our characters–for I've remarked your wife is jealous, Tom.'

"'Pon my sowl, that's thrue,' says Tom, with a smirk.

"'More fool she,' says the cat, 'for, 'pon my conscience, Tom, you're as ugly as if you wor bespoke.'

"Off ran the cat with these words, leaving Tom in amazement; he said nothing to the family for fear of fright'ning them, and off he went to the *town* as he *pretended*–for he saw the cat watching him through a hole in the hedge; but when he came to a turn at the end of the road, the dickins a mind he minded the market, good or bad, but went off to Squire Botherum's, the magisthrit, to sware examinations agin the cat.

"'Pooh! pooh! nonsense;'–broke in the little man, who had listened thus far to Murtough with an expression of mingled wonder and contempt, while the rest of the party willingly gave up the reins to nonsense, and enjoyed Murtough's legend, and their companions more absurd common sense.

"'Don't interrupt him, Goggins,' said Mister Wiggins.

"'How can you listen to such nonsense?' returned Goggins. 'Swear examinations against a cat, indeed, pooh! pooh!'

"'My dear sir,' said Murtough, 'remember this is a fairy story, and that the country all around here is full of enchantment. As I was telling you, Tom went off to swear examinations.

"''Aye, aye;' shouted all but Goggins; 'go on with the story.'

"And when Tom was asked to relate the events of the morning, which brought him before Squire Botherum, his brain was so bewildered between his corn, and his cat, and his child's toe, that he made a very confused account of it.

"'Begin your story from the beginning,' said the magistrate to Tom.

"'Well, your honour,' says Tom, 'I was goin' to market this mornin' to sell the child's corn–I beg your pard'n–my own toes, I mane, sir.'

"'Sell your toes?' said the squire.

"'No, sir, takin' the cat to market, I mane–'

"'Take a cat to market?' said the squire–'you're drunk, man.'

"'No, your honour, only confused a little; for when the toes began to spake to me–the cat, I mane–I was bothered clane.'

"'The cat spake to you?' said the squire; 'phew,–worse than before; you're drunk, Tom.'

"'No, your honour; it's on the strength of the cat I come to spake to you–'

"'I think it's on the strength of a pint o' whiskey, Tom.'

"'By the vartue o' my oath, your honour, it's nothing but the cat.'

"And so Tom then told him all about the affair, and the squire was regularly astonished. Just then, the bishop of the diocese, and the priest of the parish happened to call in, and heard the story; and the bishop, and the priest, had a tough argument for two hours on the subject; the former swearing she must be a witch–but the priest denying *that*, and maintaining she was only enchanted–and that part of the argument was afterwards referred to the primate, and subsequently to the conclave at Rome; but the pope declined interfering about cats, saying he had quite enough to do, minding his own bulls.

"'In the meantime, what are we to do with the cat?' says Botherum.

"'Burn her,' says the bishop; 'she's a witch.'

"'*Only* enchanted,' said the priest–'and the ecclesiastical court maintains that–'

"'Bother the ecclesiastical court!' said the magistrate; 'I can only proceed on the statutes;' and with that he pulled down all the law-books in his library, and hunted the laws from Queen Elizabeth down, and he found that they made laws against everything in Ireland, except a cat.–The devil a thing escaped them but a cat, which did not come within the meaning of any act of parliament:–*the cats only had escaped.*

"'There's the alien act, to be sure,' said the magistrate, and perhaps she's a French spy, in disguise.'

"'She spakes like a French spy, sure enough,' says Tom; and she was missin', I remember, all last Spy-Wednesday.'

"'That's suspicious,' says the squire–but conviction might be difficult; and I have a fresh idea,' says Botherum.

"'Faith, it won't keep fresh long, this hot weather,' says Tom; so your honour had betther make use of it at wanst.'

"'Right,' says Botherum–'we'll make her subject to the game laws; we'll hunt her,' say he.

"'Ow!-iligant!' says Tom; we'll have a brave run out of her.'

"'Meet me at the cross-roads,' says the squire, 'in the morning, and I'll have the hounds ready.'

"Well, off Tom went home; and he was racking his brain what excuse he could make to the cat for not bringing the shoes; and at last he hit one off just as he saw her cantering up to him, half a mile before he got home.

"'Where's the shoes, Tom?' says she.

"'I have not got them to-day, ma'am,' says he.

"'Is that the way you keep your promise, Tom?' says she; 'I'll tell you what it is, Tom–I'll tear the eyes out o' the childre', if you don't get me shoes–'

"'Whist! whist!' says Tom, frightened out of his life for his children's eyes. Don't be in a passion, pussey. The shoemaker said he had not a shoe in his shop, nor a last that would make one to fit you; and he says, I must bring you into the town for him to take your measure.'

"'And when am I to go?' says the cat, looking savage. 'To-morrow,' says Tom.

"'It's well you said that, Tom,' says the cat, or the divil an eye I'd lave in your family this night,' and off she hopped.

"Tom thrimbled at the wicked look she gave.

"'Remember!' says she, over the hedge, with a bitter caterwaul.

"'Never fear,' says Tom.

"Well, sure enough, the next mornin', there was the cat at cock-crow, licking herself as nate as a new pin, to go into the town, and out came Tom, with a bag undher his arm, and the cat afther him.

"'Now, git into this, and I'll carry you into the town,' says Tom, opening the bag.

"'Sure I can walk with you,' says the cat.

"'Oh, that wouldn't do,' says Tom; the people in the town is curious and slandherous people, and sure it would rise ugly remarks if I was seen with a cat afther me:–a dog is a man's companion by nature, but cats does not stand to rayson.'

"Well, the cat seeing there was no use in argument, got into the bag, and off Tom set to the cross-roads, with the bag over his shoulder, and he came up, *quite innocent-like*, to the corner, where the squire and his huntsman, and the hounds, and a pack o' people were waitin'. Out came the squire on a sudden, just as if it was all by accident.

"'God save you, Tom,' says he.

"'God save you kindly, sir,' says Tom.

"'What's that bag you have at your back?' says the squire.

"'Oh, nothin' at all, sir,' says Tom–makin' a face all the time, as much as to say, 'I have her safe.'

"'Oh, there's something in that bag, I think,' says the squire, 'and you must let me see it.'

"'If you bethray me, Tom Connor,' says the cat in a low voice, 'by this and that I'll never spake to you again!'

"'Pon my honour, sir,' says Tom, with a wink, and a twitch of his thumb towards the bag–'I haven't anything in it.'

"'I have been missing my praties of late,' says the squire, 'and I'd just like to examine that bag,' says he.

"'Is it doubtin' my characther, you'd be, sir?' says Tom, pretending to be in a passion.

"'Tom, your sowl!' says the voice in the sack, '*if you let the cat out of the bag*, I'll murther you.'

"'An honest man would make no objection to be searched,' said the squire, 'and I insist on it,' says he, laying hold o' the bag, and Tom pretending to fight all the time; but, my jewel! before two minutes, they shook the cat out o' the bag, sure enough, and off she went with her tail as big as a sweeping brush, and the squire, with a thundering view halloo, after her, clapt the dogs at her heels, and away they went for the bare life. Never was there seen such running as that day–the cat made for a shaking bog, the loneliest place in the whole counthry–and there the riders were all thrown out, barrin' the huntsman, who had a web-footed horse on purpose for soft places; and the priest, whose horse could go anywhere by rayson of the priest's blessing; and sure enough, the huntsman and his rivirence stuck to the hunt like wax; and just as the cat got on the border of the bog, they saw her give a twist as the foremost dog closed with her, for he gave her a nip in the flank. Still she went on, however, and headed them well, towards an old mud cabin in the middle of the bog, and there they saw her jump in at the window, and up came the dogs the next minit, and gathered round the house with the most horrid howling ever was heard. The huntsman alighted, and went into the house to turn the cat out again–when what should he see but an old hag, lying in bed in the corner–

"'Ow, ow! you owld divil–is it you? you owld cat?' says he, opening the door.

"In rushed the dogs–up jumped the old hag, and changing into a cat before their eyes, out she darted through the window again, and made another run for it; but she couldn't escape, and the dogs gobbled her while you would say Jack Robinson.' But the most remarkable part of this extraordinary story, gentlemen, is, that the pack was ruined from that day out; for after having eaten the enchanted cat, *the divil a thing they would ever hunt afterwards, but mice.*"—Handy Andy.

Elizabeth F. Ellet
(1818-1877)

Introduction
"The Witch Caprusche "

Elizabeth ("Lummis") Ellet was born in 1818 and became a writer in her late teens and twenties. She continued to write until her death in 1877. Originality was the Achilles heel of Ellet in her fictional works. That's why it is not surprising she admits in the preamble to "The Witch Caprusche," her best fantasy story, that the overarching idea is not of her own creation. She attributes it to a "household tale" of Denmark and it is set in the age of the vikings.

Ellet is, perhaps, best known today for the scandal she brought in relation to Edgar Allan Poe's rumored affair with Frances Sargent Osgood while both were married to other people. That is never a good sign for an author. Seeking revenge for the scandal Ellet brought into his life, Edgar Allan Poe references the "wholesale plagiarism" for which Ellet had been charged. Though refusing to believe it, the mere reference by Poe caused the damage. Poe admits that he has little interest in her works and closed the piece by referring to her as short and fat.

"Mrs. ELLETT, or ELLET, has been long before the public as an author. Having contributed largely to the newspapers and other periodicals in her youth, she first made her debût on a more comprehensive scale, as the writer of "Teresa Contarini," in a five-act tragedy, which had considerable merit, but was withdrawn after its first night of representation at the Park. This occurred at some period previous to the year 1834; the precise date I am unable to remember. The ill success of the play had little effect in repressing the ardor of the poetess, who has since furnished numerous papers to the Magazines. Her articles are, for the most part, in the *rifacimento* way, and, although no doubt composed in good faith, have the disadvantage of looking as if hashed up for just so much money as they will bring. The charge of wholesale plagiarism which has been adduced against Mrs. Ellett, I confess that I have not felt sufficient interest in her works, to investigate—and am therefore bound to believe it unfounded. In person, short and much included to embonpoint."

True originality aside, Ellet "the reconstructionist" penned one of the best witch stories for the first half of the 19th century in "The Witch Caprusche." This was certainly to the dismay of Poe. It is a short tale, but full of good characters that must be attributed to Ellet. She published it in *The Columbian Lady's and Gentlemen's Magazine* during August of 1845 where her name was listed as "Mrs. E. F. Ellett." The *Tribune* newspaper of New York called the story "a singularly wild and beautiful legend." Five years later Ellet would republish the story in the collection she edited, *Popular Legends; or, Evenings at Woodlawn.*

Ellet tried all forms and variations of writing, ultimately becoming best known for her non-fiction book, "The Women of the American Revolution," published in 1848. This was three years after she published "The Witch Caprusche." This not the first time I have published it. In *Middle Unearthed: The Best Fantasy Short Stories 1800-1849* anthology, I also included Ellet's bewitching story and "Nosey, the Dwarf" by Whilhelm Hauf. The latter story is also an excellent witch story and is worth a read.

The Witch Caprusche
1845

"Toke Jarl" has been called the Danish "Macbeth;" and indeed resembles, in his ambition and evil fate, the king whom Shakespeare has immortalized. In other respects, the story is different. The following is the legend as it is current throughout Denmark; familiar as a household tale among the people, though never recorded in any lasting work.

IN THE DARK ages, when Paganism ruled over the land and the light even of civilization but faintly shone, there lived a king in Denmark whose name has not descended to later times. Yet he governed a fair country and possessed much power. At the period of this story he was in the decline of life and had been twenty years a widower. His only child was a daughter, the beautiful Ruscha, whose mother had died in giving her birth.

In all of the neighboring kingdoms the fame of princess Ruscha's beauty was widely spread; and many were the noble suitors for her hand. But the princess was proud and imperious as fair. She rejected every proposal of marriage and treated her lovers with so much scorn that almost all were incited to hate and speak ill of her. She thus raised up enemies on every side.

The old king was much incensed at this conduct and sharply reproved his daughter. "Was it not enough," he said—"that you would not choose of one of your suitors—but they must be repulsed with such bitter contempt? Your haughty bearing and evil tongue have converted these friends into foes. Murmur not, therefore, at what I will do. I am old and feeble. A few years—and I must depart from this earth to take my place among the heroes of Valhalla and drink the mead of Odin. You are young, and a woman. Who will shield you when I am gone from the powerful warriors—your enemies? By the hammer of Thor do I swear, you will choose a husband—who may be your protector and king in my place. If you still refuse to do this I swear by Odin's golden horn, out of which heroes drink, I will name me a successor! I will not suffer you, ungrateful girl, to rule my people according to your own capricious will!"

When the king had spoken, he went out leaving the princess alone. Her face was crimson with anger, and her blue eyes flashed resentment. She paced the room for some time with unquiet steps; for the thought that the sovereignty might be wrested from her was too painful for her to bear. At length she threw herself into a seat and sat long with her fair head drooped on her hands. Then starting up, as if she had suddenly formed a resolution, she retired to her own apartment.

For many days after the old king showed much severity toward his daughter and his harsh rebukes were frequent. At length she informed him she was willing to choose a consort.

"Let all the neighboring princes and nobles and those who have sought me in marriage," she said, "be invited to the court—that I may make choice among them."

But her father answered, "Not so, by Odin and Frela! The princes and nobles of the neighboring countries have no longer any pleasure in you! I counsel you to choose one of your own kinsmen. What about Bue, the stout, or Eric—or Swed, the squinter?"

The princess curled her haughty lip in scorn and answered not. But after some days she signified her choice. The person she selected was not among her rejected suitors. It was Toke Jarl, surnamed the slender. He was of princely descent, possessed a large patrimony of land and was moreover distinguished for courage and manly beauty. He was richer than Ruscha's own kinsmen, so that the old king made no objections to his becoming the husband of his daughter and his declared successor. He dispatched messengers to Toke Jarl to announce to him his good fortune. Toke was well pleased with the intelligence and praised the blue eyes and the ripe judgment of the princess. He ordered some of his best horses and his finest oxen to be led as a present to the king, with thanks for the honor done him; and announced that he would the next day present himself as a suitor before the beautiful Ruscha, who should never have reason to repent her choice.

The marriage was celebrated with due splendor at the king's castle, where Toke Jarl proved himself a veritable hero; for he drank not only his father-in-law under the table, but also his cousins Bue, the stout, Eric, and Swed, the squinter without showing himself the slightest symptom of inebriation. After this achievement he took the fair bride from her maidens and led her to the nuptial chamber.

Ruscha was not happy even after her union with the object of her choice. Ambition was her ruling passion; and she longed to feel the golden circlet of royalty on her brows, even before it could lawfully become hers by the death of her father. An evil spirit possessed her, and she hated the good old king from the day he had so harshly reproved her and proposed a marriage with one of her cousins.

She knew that Toke Jarl loved her passionately and resolved to make him her instrument for the gratification of her wicked desires. She assumed a deep melancholy—and a grief-worn aspect—as if she shed many tears in secret. "What ails you, Ruscha?" he would ask, and she would not reply. Then Toke would swear by Thor and Odin that if anyone had vexed her he would die.

The cunning princess wept more bitterly, and whispered, "Could you take away the life of the king, my father, and escape the infamy of being called his murderer?"

Toke Jarl started and looked earnestly and gloomily on his wife.

"It is the king," she continued, "who torments me day by day. I must die if he is suffered to live. Know also, Toke, that he is about to disinherit me and you, and to declare Eric his successor."

The brow of Toke Jarl grew black. "You have said it!" he exclaimed. "It will be done!" And he went out hastily.

The same day one of his slaves, a Finlander by birth, stole from the armory of Eric an arrow marked with his name. Toke Jarl went forth into the woods with this arrow, where the king was accustomed to hunt.

At evening when the monarch did not return, men were dispatched in search of him. They found his corpse in the wood, the arrow buried in his side. The body was brought back with loud lamentations. The people ran tumultuously to the palace gates. Every one recognized the arrow, and the cry was, "Eric, the bloody Eric, has slain our good king! Death to the murderer!"

Toke Jarl dispatched officers to arrest his wife's cousin and had his head stricken off in the sight of all. Then he was proclaimed king and solemnly crowned, with Ruscha his wife.

The guilty pair were now at the height they had longed to reach; but happiness came not with power. On the contrary, both grew every day more gloomy and dejected, and each distrusted the other. If the queen had no scruples to doom her own father to death, thought Toke Jarl, much less would she hesitate to foster my destruction! And Ruscha reflected with equal reason, that he who had basely taken away an old man's life at her prompting, would as readily sacrifice her whenever his love should be transferred to another. They looked on each other therefore with suspicion; the king watching closely every word and action of his consort, and jealously preventing her from any interference in the concerns of the kingdom, lest she should win from him the hearts of the people.

The queen hated her husband more and more every day and would gladly have rid herself of him but that she feared to undertake any deed of violence. The people loved their young sovereign who ruled them wisely though he was severe even to cruelty in matters of punishment.

Ruscha, however, was deceitful and cunning, and pondered day and night on the means of accomplishing her wishes without drawing suspicion on herself. One day she wandered alone in the forest, in the depths of which dwelt an old woman, whom common rumor accused of dealings with evil spirits of the wood. The virtuous feared and shunned her, but the queen now sought her out and was not long in finding her. The old woman was picking up sticks. She looked up as she saw her fair young visitor and a smile curled her withered lips.

"I am the queen," said Ruscha coming at once to the object of her visit. "I seek your aid against Toke Jarl, my husband."

"What has he done?" asked the witch.

"He practices treason against my life. I would he be dead before I band with him."

The old woman dropped her bundle of sticks, and stood upright, looking full into the eyes of the queen. "I can do nothing for you," she said "till you form a compact with me and those with whom I am leagued. You must sign the compact and give me your blood. Then will your veins be filled with the fire that animates immortal spirits and you will never taste of death."

"Will you promise me then, revenge on Toke Jarl?" Ruscha asked, her blue eyes flashing fire.

The old woman nodded.

"Then I will comply with your conditions," said the queen; and the wood-witch led the way to a cave hidden from sight by very thick bushes and foliage that shut out the beams of sun even at noon-day.

Within the recesses of this cave the deep darkness was rendered more horrible by hideous shapes that flashed like tongues of flame before the eyes, and by the sullen glare of the fire over which hung the caldron of infernal preparations. When the queen reappeared from that den of demons, a change had taken place in her looks. Her skin before so delicately fair, had a strange dazzling glow, as if tinged with the reflection of sunset. Her eyes were much darker and flashed with almost intolerable brightness. With a light step and joy in her face she returned to the city and the palace, having promised before she parted with the witch to visit her on the seventeenth day of every month to renew the league into which they had entered.

From that hour king Toke Jarl was attacked with illness. During the day he suffered not, but as soon as night came, the most agonizing pains tortured him in all his limbs. It seemed to him as if molten metal, instead of blood, flowed through his veins. The anguish was so intense that it threatened to destroy him. He grew every day more emaciated, and wandered like a spectre about his palace. All the science of his physicians availed nothing.

The little Finnish slave, hopeless of relief for his master from ordinary means, determined on a desperate remedy. He went through the woods, and reaching the mountains, gathered herbs in the moonlight from which he prepared a drink and administered it to the king, who lay helpless on his couch and knew not what was done to him. After a while the pain abated. Toke Jarl rose up in bed and looked around him. "What has been done to me?" he asked.

The Finnish slave threw himself on his knees before the king. "My gracious lord," he cried, "I know now what is your malady! I have sought the most poisonous herbs impregnated by the moonbeams and banned by evil spirits and distilled them into a drink of which you have taken. The potion has done you no harm, but driven away your pains. This would not have happened had your malady been a natural one. Now I know that my lord the king is bewitched and I know moreover that if he had not means to break the spell, his life will have been sacrificed and the land will have to seek another ruler."

Toke Jarl sprang in horror from his couch. "By Thor's hammer and the horn of Odin I swear," he cried, "if you will help me discover who has done me this evil turn, from that hour you will be free, and the highest noble at my court!"

But the boy quietly seated himself on the footstool by the royal couch and answered, "My lord and master, I would always remain your slave and servant, and receive from your hands my wheat bread and honey, and cured bear's flesh and as much old mead as I can drink. May this be, I will speak my whole mind."

Toke Jarl nodded, and the boy went on: "Consider, my lord, how long it is since this bad demon had power over you! Was it not from that very night when my royal lady the queen was missing all day from the palace and returned late, saying she had lost herself in the wood? Has she not three times since wandered in the same wood, and been lost, and returned at night? By all your gods, my king, and their horns and their hammers, of which I know nothing, I do believe that my lady, the queen, knows but too well the way to the dwelling of the old witch Runna, who can conjure all the wood spirits, and has for a servant, a dark looking elf, a little demon with red tongue always hanging out of his mouth!"

The king grew paler and paler while his servant was speaking. Then he seated himself on the side of the bed and mused awhile. At length he said, "You are right! Yes, I do believe you are right! May all good and evil spirits help me to take vengeance on my faithless wife! Tell me, boy, have you observed when the day returns?"

"The day after tomorrow, my lord."

"It is well; and the hour, do you know it?"

"I do, my lord! We will follow the queen and hear what she will say to old Runna."

"Well said, boy. Now give me another draught of your poison drink that I may go to sleep. That golden horn over there is full of excellent mead. Drink to my health."

Griep administered to the king another draught of the medicine and the monarch fell into a slumber, while the boy crouched on the low stool, sipped the mead from the golden horn and pleased himself with the prospect of abundance of honey, wheat bread and bear's flesh.

The next day and the following, queen Ruscha observed that the king gained strength visibly in spite of the power of her spell. The poison draught of the little Griep had restored him.

Her dismay was excessive. She longed impatiently for the seventh hour of the evening, and as soon as the West was crimson with sunset she departed, attired in a plain dress and her face concealed by a veil. She left the city and with steps trembling from eagerness hastened into the forest.

Griep led the king also by a secret and shorter path through the wood close to the old witch's cave. There, hidden among the bushes but near enough to hear all that was said, they awaited the arrival of the queen.

Ruscha came at length, stood before the cave and called, "Runna!" three times. At the third call a sullen rumbling noise was heard within the cavern. The iron door, which had been closed, opened slowly and the old witch appeared. "What do you want?" she asked.

"Help!" cried Ruscha. "Your spell has no longer any effect. For the last three days Toke Jarl has been on the recovery. In vain every night, by your direction, I have strewed coals around his waxen image and enveloped it in poisonous vapors. He has seemed yesterday and today stronger than ever!"

The hag knit her brows. "If it be as you say, there must be a counter spell at work more potent than mine. If this avails not, you must deprive the king of life at once."

"And lose the pleasure of tormenting him?" cried the evil queen. "But how can it be done?"

The witch laughed bitterly, for she was piqued at the failure of her magic in the first instance. "Were he a hero as mighty as the great Thor himself," she said, "he must yield to the word of power which I will give you."

Ruscha's eyes sparkled. "Oh, give it to me, good Runna!" she exclaimed.

Runna pronounced the word of power. The king listened breathlessly "When you meet Toke Jarl," continued the witch, "fix your eyes steadily upon his. Utter the word and call him by name. He will fall instantly, struck down by its magic. Now, fare-thee-well! My spirits summon me!"

The witch vanished and Ruscha turned from the cave on her way homewards. At the entrance of the wood she suddenly encountered the king standing in a threatening attitude, with his drawn sword uplifted. She started back with a scream of terror; but with scornful mockery he shouted the word given her by Runna, adding her own name and at the same time dealt her a furious blow with the sword, which cleft her head. Ruscha sank to the ground.

Toke Jarl fled to his castle, wiping the blood from his sword with his hand. Then he returned it to its sheath. Soon his hand began to burn, as if scorched with fire. In vain he plunged it into water and moist earth. The horrible burning extended to his arm, gradually spreading over his whole body, and before many hours elapsed he expired in dreadful torments.

Ruscha could not die, as the witch had assured her, nor could she live like the other inhabitants of earth. To this day it is said she wanders about her native country, a being who belongs neither to the living nor the dead. Many persons have averred that she has been seen wandering at night, in white fluttering garments, with face beautiful but ghastly pale, her veil red with blood that continually flows from the gaping wound in her head.

Old and young in Denmark believe in her existence, and that she sometimes appears. From the circumstance that the "word of power" given her by Runna, was supposed to sound like "Cap" that has become the popular prefix to her name and she is universally known as the fair but evil witch Caprusche.

James Hogg
(1770–1835)

Introduction
"The Brownie of the Black Haggs"

James Hogg, a well-regarded Scottish poet, author and essayist was raised in a poor family. As a young man he worked as a farmhand, often tending sheep. He was given the "Ettrick Shepherd" as a nickname because he watched over sheep near the Ettrick Water in Ettrick, Scotland. Self-educated, he soon began writing poetry with a bend toward the supernatural and witchcraft.

In 1813, at the age of forty three, Hogg published "The Queen's Wake," a long narrative poetic work that included a number of poems, including "The Witch of Fife." One biographer deemed it "a gem from the realms of witchcraft, and shows in a wonderful manner Hogg's vein of thought and imagination. It is a strange, grotesque description of lawless doings with the evil one. Full of nice humour and caustic wit, blended with finely painted descriptions of scenes of nature through which the witches passed in their flight . . ..."

Nearly fifteen years later, approaching the age of sixty, the Ettrick Shepherd published the biting short story "The Brownie of the Black Haggs." A brownie is a household spirit that appears at night while the owners of the house are asleep to perform various chores. The human owners of the house must leave a reward for the brownie on the fireplace hearth. Brownies are easily angered and known to conduct pranks in the house. "The Brownie of the Black Haggs" is filled with Scottish brogue and modern readers must read it slowly. It is worth every second for the oldest witch story in this collection.

Hogg died in November 1835 and was buried in the Ettrick Churchyard. He was a friend of Sir Walter Scott and William Wordsworth. The latter issued a eulogy on the death of James Hogg with the lines:

The mighty Minstrel breathes no longer,
'Mid mouldering ruins low he lies;
And death upon the braes of Yarrow,
Has closed the Shepherd-poet's eyes.

The Brownie of the Black Haggs
1827

WHEN THE SPROTS were lairds of Wheelhope, which is now a long time ago, there was one of the ladies who was very badly spoken of in the country. People did not just openly assert that Lady Wheelhope was a witch, but every one had an aversion even at hearing her named; and when by chance she happened to be mentioned, old men would shake their heads and say, "Ah! let us alane o' her! The less ye meddle wi' her the better." Auld wives would give over spinning, and, as a pretence for hearing what might be said about her, poke in the fire with the tongs, cocking up their ears all the while; and then, after some meaning coughs, hems, and haws, would haply say, "Hech-wow, sirs! An a' be true that's said!" or something equally wise and decisive as that.

In short, Lady Wheelhope was accounted a very bad woman. She was an inexorable tyrant in her family, quarrelled with her servants, often cursing them, striking them, and turning them away; especially if they were religious, for these she could not endure, but suspected them of every thing bad. Whenever she found out any of the servant men of the laird's establishment for religious characters, she soon gave them up to the military, and got them shot; and several girls that were regular in their devotions, she was supposed to have popped off with poison. She was certainly a wicked woman, else many good people were mistaken in her character, and the poor persecuted Covenanters were obliged to unite in their prayers against her.

As for the laird, he was a stump. A big, dun-faced, pluffy body, that cared neither for good nor evil, and did not well know the one from the other. He laughed at his lady's tantrums and barley-hoods; and the greater the rage that she got into, the laird thought it the better sport. One day, when two servant maids came running to him, in great agitation, and told him that his lady had felled one of their companions, the laird laughed heartily at them, and said he did not doubt it.

"Why, sir, how can you laugh?" said they. "The poor girl is killed."

"Very likely, very likely," said the laird. "Well, it will teach her to take care who she angers again."

"And, sir, your lady will be hanged."

"Very likely; well, it will learn her how to strike so rashly again—Ha, ha, ha! Will it not, Jessy?"

But when this same Jessy died suddenly one morning, the laird was greatly confounded, and seemed dimly to comprehend that there had been unfair play going. There was little doubt that she was taken off by poison; but whether the lady did it through jealousy or not, was never divulged: but it greatly bamboozled and astonished the poor laird, for his nerves failed him, and his whole frame became paralytic. He seems to have been exactly in the same state of mind with a colley that I once had. He was extremely fond of the gun as long as I did not kill any thing with her, (there being no game laws in Ettrick Forest in those days,) and he got a grand chase after the hares when I missed them. But there was one day that I chanced for a marvel to shoot one dead, a few paces before his nose. I'll never forget the astonishment that the poor beast manifested. He stared one while at the gun, and another while at the dead hare, and seemed to be drawing the conclusion, that if the case stood thus, there was no creature sure of its life. Finally, he took his tail between his legs, and ran away home, and never would face a gun all his life again.

So was it precisely with Laird Sprot of Wheelhope. As long as his lady's wrath produced only noise and splutter among the servants, he thought it fine sport: but when he saw what he believed the dreadful effects of it, he became like a barrel organ out of tune, and could only discourse one note, which he did to every one he met. "I wish she maunna hae gotten something she has been the waur of." This note he repeated early and late, night and day, sleeping and waking, alone and in company, from the moment that Jessy died till she was buried; and on going to the churchyard as chief mourner, he whispered it to her relations by the way. When they came to the grave, he took his stand at the head, nor would he give place to the girl's father; but there he stood, like a huge post, as though he neither saw nor heard; and when he had lowered her late comely head into the grave, and dropped the cord, he slowly lifted his hat with one hand, wiped his dim eyes with the back of the other, and said, in a deep tremulous tone, "Poor lassie! I wish she didna get something she had been the waur of."

This death made a great noise among the common people; but there was no protection for the life of the subject in those days; and provided a man or woman was a true loyal subject, and a real Anti-Covenanter, any of them might kill as many as they liked. So there was no one to take cognizance of the circumstances relating to the death of poor Jessy.

After this, the lady walked softly for the space of two or three years. She saw that she had rendered herself odious, and had entirely lost her husband's countenance, which she liked worst of all. But the evil propensity could not be overcome; and a poor boy, whom the laird, out of sheer compassion, had taken into his service, being found dead one morning, the country people could no longer be restrained; so they went in a body to the Sheriff, and insisted on an investigation. It was proved that she detested the boy, had often threatened him, and had given him brose and butter the afternoon before he died; but the cause was ultimately dismissed, and the pursuers fined.

No one can tell to what height of wickedness she might now have proceeded, had not a check of a very singular kind been laid upon her. Among the servants that came home at the next term, was one who called himself Merodach: and a strange person he was. He had the form of a boy, but the features of one a hundred years old, save that his eyes had a brilliancy and restlessness, which was very extraordinary, bearing a strong resemblance to the eyes of a well-known species of monkey. He was froward and perverse in all his actions, and disregarded the pleasure or displeasure of any person; but he performed his work well, and with apparent ease. From the moment that he entered the house, the lady conceived a mortal antipathy against him, and besought the laird to turn him away. But the laird, of himself, never turned away any body, and moreover he had hired him for a trivial wage, and the fellow neither wanted activity nor perseverance. The natural consequence of this arrangement was, that the lady instantly set herself to make Merodach's life as bitter as it was possible, in order to get early quit of a domestic every way so disgusting. Her hatred of him was not like a common antipathy entertained by one human being against another,—she hated him as one might hate a toad or an adder: and his occupation of jotteryman (as the laird termed his servant of all work) keeping him always about her hand, it must have proved highly disagreeable.

She scolded him, she raged at him, but he only mocked her wrath, and giggled and laughed at her, with the most provoking derision. She tried to fell him again and again, but never, with all her address, could she hit him; and never did she make a blow at him, that she did not repent it. She was heavy and unwieldy, and he as quick in his motions as a monkey; besides, he generally had her in such an ungovernable rage, that when she flew at him, she hardly knew what she was doing. At one time she guided her blow towards him, and he at the same instant avoided it with such dexterity, that she knocked down the chief hind, or foresman; and then Merodach giggled so heartily, that, lifting the kitchen poker, she threw it at him with a full design of knocking out his brains; but the missile only broke every plate and ashet on the kitchen dresser.

She then hasted to the laird, crying bitterly, and telling him she would not suffer that wretch Merodach, as she called him, to stay another night in the family. "Why, then, put him away, and trouble me no more about him," said the laird.

"Put him away!" exclaimed she; "I have already ordered him away a hundred times, and charged him never to let me see his horrible face again; but he only flouts me, and tells me he'll see me at the devil first."

The pertinacity of the fellow amused the laird exceedingly; his dim eyes turned upwards into his head with delight: he then looked two ways at once, turned round his back, and laughed till the tears ran down his dun cheeks, but he could only articulate "You're fitted now."

The lady's agony of rage still increasing from this derision, she flew on the laird, and said he was not worthy the name of a man, if he did not turn away that pestilence, after the way he had abused her.

"Why, Shusy, my dear, what has he done to you?"

"What done to me! has he not caused me to knock down John Thomson, and I do not know if ever he will come to life again?"

"Have you felled your favourite John Thomson?" said the laird, laughing more heartily than before: "you might have done a worse deed than that. But what evil has John done?"

"And has he not broke every plate and dish on the whole dresser?" continued the lady, disregarding the laird's question: "and for all this devastation, he only mocks at my displeasure, absolutely mocks me, and if you do not have him turned away, and hanged or shot for his deeds, you are not worthy the name of man."

"O alack! What a devastation among the china metal!" said the laird: and calling on Merodach, he said, "Tell me, thou evil Merodach of Babylon, how thou dared'st knock down thy lady's favourite servant, John Thomson?"

"Not I, your honour. It was my lady herself, who got into such a furious rage at me, that she mistook her man, and felled Mr Thomson: and the good man's skull is fractured."

"That was very odd," said the laird, chuckling; "I do not comprehend it. But then, what the devil set you on smashing all my lady's delft and china ware?—That was a most infamous and provoking action."

"It was she herself, your honour. Sorry would I have been to have broken one dish belonging to the house. I take all the house-servants to witness, that my lady smashed all the dishes with a poker, and now lays the blame on me."

The laird turned his dim and delighted eyes on his lady, who was crying with vexation and rage, and seemed meditating another personal attack on the culprit, which he did not at all appear to shun, but rather encourage. She, however, vented her wrath in threatenings of the most deep and desperate revenge, the creature all the while assuring her that she would be foiled, and that in all her encounters and contests with him, she would uniformly come to the worst. He was resolved to do his duty, and there before his master he defied her.

The laird thought more than he considered it prudent to reveal; but he had little doubt that his wife would wreak that vengeance on his jotteryman which she avowed, and as little of her capability. He almost shuddered when he recollected one who had taken something that she had been the waur of.

In a word, the Lady of 'Wheelhope's inveterate malignity against this one object, was like the rod of Moses, that swallowed up the rest of the serpents. All her wicked and evil propensities seemed to be superseded by it, if not utterly absorbed in its virtues. The rest of the family now lived in comparative peace and quietness; for early and late her malevolence was venting itself against the jotteryman, and him alone. It was a delirium of hatred and vengeance, on which the whole bent and bias of her inclination was set. She could not stay from the creature's presence, for in the intervals when absent from him, she spent her breath in curses and execrations, and then not able to rest, she ran again to seek him, her eyes gleaming with the anticipated delights of vengeance, while, ever and anon, all the scaith, the ridicule, and the harm, redounded on herself.

Was it not strange that she could not get quit of this sole annoyance of her life? One would have thought she easily might. But by this time there was nothing farther from her intention: she wanted vengeance, full, adequate, and delicious vengeance, on her audacious opponent. But he was a strange and terrible creature, and the means of retaliation came always, as it were, to his hand.

Bread and sweet milk was the only fare that Merodach cared for, and he having bargained for that, would not want it, though he often got it with a curse and with ill will. The lady having intentionally kept back his wonted allowance for some days, on the Sabbath morning following, she set him down a bowl of rich sweet milk, well drugged with a deadly poison, and then she lingered in a little anteroom to watch the success of her grand plot, and prevent any other creature from tasting of the potion. Merodach came in, and the housemaid says to him, "There is your breakfast, creature."

"Oho! my lady has been liberal this morning," said he; "but I am beforehand with her.—Here, little Missie, you seem very hungry to-day—take you my breakfast." And with that he set the beverage down to the lady's little favourite spaniel. It so happened that the lady's only son came at that instant into the anteroom, seeking her, and teazing his mamma about something which took her attention from the hall-table for a space. When she looked again, and saw Missie lapping up the sweet milk, she burst from her lobby like a dragon, screaming as if her head had been on fire, kicked the bowl and the remainder of its contents against the wall, and lifting Missie in her bosom, she retreated hastily, crying all the way.

"Ha, ha, ha—I have you now!" cried Merodach, as she vanished from the hall.

Poor Missie died immediately, and very privately; indeed, she would have died and been buried, and never one have seen her, save her mistress, had not Merodach, by a luck that never failed him, popped his nose over the flower garden wall, just as his lady was laying her favourite in a grave of her own digging. She, not perceiving her tormentor, plied on at her task, apostrophizing the insensate little carcass, "Ah! poor dear little creature, thou hast had a hard fortune, and hast drank of the bitter potion that was not intended for thee; but he shall drink it three times double, for thy sake!"

"Is that little Missie?" said the eldrich voice of the jotteryman, close at the lady's ear. She uttered a loud scream, and sunk down on the bank. "Alack for poor little Missie!" continued the creature in a tone of mockery, "My heart is sorry for Missie. What has befallen her—whose breakfast cup did she drink?"

"Hence with thee, thou fiend!" cried the lady: "what right hast thou to intrude on thy mistress's privacy? Thy turn is coming yet, or may the nature of woman change within me."

"It is changed already," said the creature, grinning with delight; "I have thee now, I have thee now! And were it not to shew my superiority over thee, which I do every hour, I should soon see thee strapped like a mad cat, or a worrying bratch. What wilt thou try next?"

"I will cut thy throat, and if I die for it, will rejoice in the deed; a deed of charity to all that dwell on the face of the earth. Go about thy business."

"I have warned thee before, dame, and I now warn thee again, that all thy mischief meditated against me will fall double on thine own head."

"I want none of your warning, and none of your instructions, fiendish cur. Hence with your elvish face, and take care of yourself."

It would be too disgusting and horrible to relate or read all the incidents that fell out between this unaccountable couple. Their enmity against each other had no end, and no mitigation; and scarcely a single day passed over on which her acts of malevolent ingenuity did not terminate fatally for some favourite thing of the lady's, while all these doings never failed to appear as her own act. Scarcely was there a thing, animate or inanimate, on which she set a value, left to her, that was not destroyed; and yet scarcely one hour or minute could she remain absent from her tormentor, and all the while, it seems, solely for the purpose of tormenting him.

But while all the rest of the establishment enjoyed peace and quietness from the fury of their termagant dame, matters still grew worse and worse between the fascinated pair. The lady haunted the menial, in the same manner as the raven haunts the eagle, for a perpetual quarrel, though the former knows that in every encounter she is to come off the loser. But now noises were heard on the stairs by night, and it was whispered among the menials, that the lady had been seeking Merodach's bed by night, on some horrible intent. Several of them would have sworn that they had seen her passing and repassing on the stair after midnight, when all was quiet; but then it was likewise well known, that Merodach slept with well fastened doors, and a companion in another bed in the same room, whose bed, too, was nearest the door. Nobody cared much what became of the jotteryman, for he was an unsocial and disagreeable person; but some one told him what they had seen, and hinted a suspicion of the lady's intent. But the creature only bit his upper lip, winked with his eyes, and said, "She had better let alone; she will be the first to rue that."

Not long after this, to the horror of the family and the whole country side, the laird's only son was found murdered in his bed one morning, under circumstances that manifested the most fiendish cruelty and inveteracy on the part of his destroyer. As soon as the atrocious act was divulged, the lady fell into convulsions, and lost her reason; and happy had it been for her had she never recovered either the use of reason, or her corporeal functions any more, for there was blood upon her hand, which she took no care to conceal, and there was too little doubt that it was the blood of her own innocent and beloved boy, the sole heir and hope of the family.

This blow deprived the laird of all power of action: but the lady had a brother, a man of the law, who came and instantly proceeded to an investigation of this unaccountable murder; but before the Sheriff arrived, the housekeeper took the lady's brother aside, and told him he had better not go on with the scrutiny, for she was sure the crime would be brought home to her unfortunate mistress; and after examining into several corroborative circumstances, and viewing the state of the raving maniac, with the blood on her hand and arm, he made the investigation a very short one, declaring the domestics all exculpated.

The laird attended his boy's funeral, and laid his head in the grave, but appeared exactly like a man walking in a trance, an automaton, without feelings or sensations, often times gazing at the funeral procession, as on something he could not comprehend. And when the death-bell of the parish church fell a-tolling, as the corpse approached the kirk-stile, he cast a dim eye up towards the belfry, and said hastily, "What, what's that? Och ay, we're just in time, just in time." And often was he hammering over the name of "Evil Merodach, King of Babylon," to himself. He seemed to have some far-fetched conception that his unaccountable jotteryman had a hand in the death of his only son, and other lesser calamities, although the evidence in favour of Merodach's innocence was as usual quite decisive.

This grievous mistake of Lady Wheelhope (for every landward laird's wife was then styled Lady) can only be accounted for, by supposing her in a state of derangement, or rather under some evil influence, over which she had no control: and to a person in such a state, the mistake was not so very unnatural. The mansion-house of Wheelhope was old and irregular. The stair had four acute turns, all the same, and four landing-places, all the same. In the uppermost chamber slept the two domestics,—Merodach in the bed farthest in, and in the chamber immediately below that, which was exactly similar, slept the young laird and his tutor, the former in the bed farthest in: and thus, in the turmoil of raging passions, her own hand made herself childless.

Merodach was expelled the family forthwith, but refused to accept of his wages, which the man of law pressed upon him, for fear of farther mischief; but he went away in apparent sullenness and discontent, no one knowing whither.

When his dismissal was announced to the lady, who was watched day and night in her chamber, the news had such an effect on her, that her whole frame seemed electrified; the horrors of remorse vanished, and another passion, which I neither can comprehend nor define, took the sole possession of her distempered spirit. "He must not go! He shall not go!" she exclaimed. "No, no, no—he shall not—he shall not he shall not!" and then she instantly set herself about making ready to follow him, uttering all the while the most diabolical expressions, indicative of anticipated vengeance. "Oh, could I but snap his nerves one by one, and birl among his vitals! Could I but slice his heart off piecemeal in small messes, and see his blood lopper and bubble, and spin away in purple slays; and then to see him grin, and grin, and grin, and grin! Oh—oh— oh How beautiful and grand a sight it would be to see him grin, and grin, and grin!" And in such a style would she run on for hours together.

She thought of nothing, she spake of nothing, but the discarded jotteryman, whom most people now began to regard as a creature that was not canny. They had seen him eat, and drink, and work like other people; still he had that about him that was not like other men. He was a boy in form, and an antediluvian in feature. Some thought he was a mule, between a Jew and an ape; some a wizard, some a kelpie, or a fairy, but most of all, that he was really and truly a Brownie. What he was I do not know, and therefore will not pretend to say; but be that as it may, in spite of locks and keys, watching and waking, the Lady of Wheelhope soon made her escape and eloped after him. The attendants, indeed, would have made oath that she was carried away by some invisible hand, for that it was impossible she could have escaped on foot like other people: and this edition of the story took in the country; but sensible people viewed the matter in another light.

As for instance, when Wattie Biythe, the laird's old shepherd, came in from the hill one morning, his wife Bessie thus accosted him. "His presence be about us, Wattie Blythe! have ye heard what has happened at the ha'? Things are aye turning waur and waur there, and it looks like as if Providence had gi'en up our laird's house to destruction. This grand estate maun now gang frae for the Sprots, for it has finished them."

"Na, na, Bessie, it isna the estate has finished the Sprots, but the Sprots that hae finished it, an' themsells into the boot. They hae been a wicked and degenerate race, an aye the langer the waur, till they hae reachewd the utmost bounds o' earthly wickedness; an it s time the deil were looking after his am,"

"Ah, Wattie Blythe, ye never said a truer say. An' that's just the very point where your story ends, and mine commences, for hasna the deil, or the faries, or the brownies, ta'en away our lady bodily, an' the haul country is running and riding in search o' her: and there is twenty hunder merks offered to the first that can find her, an' bring her safe back. They hae ta'en her away, skin an' bane, body an' soul, an' a'. Wattle!"

"Hech-wow! but that is awsome! And where is it thought they have ta'en her to, Bessie?"

"O, they hae some guess at that frae her am hints afore. It is thought they hae carried her after that Satan of a creature, wha wrought sae muckle wae about the house. It is for him they are a looking, for they ken weel, that where they get the tane they will get the tither."

"Whew! Is that the gate o't, Bessie? Why, then, the awfu' story is nouther mail-nor less than this, that the leddy has made a lopment, as they ca't, and run away after a blackgaird jotteryman. Hech-wow! wae' s me for human frailty! But that's just the gate! When aince the deil gets in the point o' his finger, he will soon have in his haul hand. Ay, he wants but a hair to make a tether of, ony day. I hae seen her a braw sonsy lass, but even then I feared she was devoted to destruction, for she aye mockit at religion, Bessie, an' that's no a good mark of a young body. An' she made a' its servants her enemies; an think you these good men's prayers were a' to blaw away i' the wind, and be nae mair regarded? Na, na, Bessie, my woman, take ye this mark baith o' our am bairns and ither folk's—If ever ye see a young body that disregards the Sabbath, and makes a mock at the ordinances o' religion, ye will never see that body come to muckle good. A braw hand she has made o' her gibes an' jeers at religion, an' her mockeries o' the poor persecuted hill-folk!—sunk down by degrees into the very dregs o' sin and misery! run away after a scullion!"

"Fy, fy, Wattie, how can ye say sac? It was wed kenn'd that she hatit him wi' a perfect an' mortal hatred, an' tried to make away wi' him mae ways nor and."

"Aha, Bessie; but nipping an' scarting are Scots folk's wooing; an' though it is but right that we suspend our judgments, there will naebody persuade me, if she be found alang wi' the creature, but that she has run away after him in the natural way, on her twa shanks, without help either frae fairy or brownie."

"I'll never believe sic a thing of any woman born, let be a lady wee' up in years."

"Od help ye, Bessie! ye dinna ken the stretch o' corrupt nature. The best o' us, when left to oursells, are nae better than strayed sheep, that will never find the way back to their am pastures; an' of a' things made o' mortal flesh, a wicked woman is the warst."

"Alack-a-day! we get the blame o' muckle that we little deserve. But, Wattie, keep ye a gayan sharp look-out about the cleuchs and the caves o' our glen, or hope, as ye ca't; for the lady kens them a gayan weel; and gin the twenty hunder merks wad come our way, it might gang a waur gate. It wad tocher a' our bonny lasses."

"Ay, weel I wat, Bessie, that's nae lee. And now, when ye bring me amind o't, the L forgie me gin I didna hear a creature up in the Brock-holes this morning, skirting as if something war cutting its throat. It gars a' the hairs stand on my head when I think it may hae been our leddy, an the droich of a creature murdering her. I took it for a battle of wulcats, and wished they might pu' out ane anither's thrapples; but when I think on it again they war unco like some o our leddys unearthly screams."

"His presence be about us, Wattie! Haste ye. Pit on your bonnet- take your staff in your hand, and gang an' see what it is."

"Shame fa' me if I daur gang, Bessie."

"Hout, Wattie, trust in the Lord."

"Aweel, sae I do. But ane's no to throw himsell ower a linn, an trust that the Lord's to kep him in a blanket; nor hing himself up in a raip, an' expect the Lord to come and cut him down. An' it's nae muckle safer for an auld stiff man to gang away out to a wild remote place, where there is ae body murdering another.—What is that I hear, Bessie? Haud the lang tongue o' you, and rin to the door, an' see what noise that is."

Bessie ran to the door, but soon returned an altered creature, with her mouth wide open, and her eyes set in her head.

"It is them, Wattie! it is them! His presence be about us! What will we do?"

"Them? whaten them?"

"Why, that blackguard creature, coming here, leading our leddy be the hair o' the head, an' yerking her wi' a stick. I am terrified out o' my wits. What will we do?"

"We'll see what they sad," said Wattie, manifestly in as great terror as his wife: and by a natural impulse, or as a last resource, he opened the Bible, not knowing what he did, and then hurried on his spectacles; but before he got two leaves turned over, the two entered, a frightful-looking couple indeed. Merodach, with his old withered face, and ferret eyes, leading the Lady of Wheelhope by the long hair, which was mixed with grey, and whose face was all bloated with wounds and bruises, and having stripes of blood on her garments.

"How's this!—How's this, sirs?" said Wattie Biythe.

"Close that book, and I will tell you, goodman," said Merodach.

"I can hear what you hae to say wi' the beuk open, sir," said Wattie, turning over the leaves, as if looking for some particular passage, but apparently not knowing what he was doing. "It is a shamefu' business this, but some will hae to answer for't. My leddy, I am unco grieved to see you in sic a plight. Ye hae surely been dooms sair left to yoursell."

The lady shook her head, uttered a feeble hollow laugh, and fixed her eyes on Merodach. But such a look! It almost frightened the simple aged couple out of their senses. It was not a look of love nor of hatred exclusively: neither was it of desire or disgust, but it was a combination of them all. It was such a look as one fiend would cast on another, in whose everlasting destruction he rejoiced. Wattie was glad to take his eyes from such countenances, and look into the Bible, that firm foundation of all his hopes and all his joy.

"I request that you will shut that book, sir," said the horrible creature; 'or if you do not, I will shut it for you with a vengeance: and with that he seized it, and flung it against the wall. Bessie uttered a scream, and Wattie was quite paralysed; and although he seemed disposed to run after his best friend, as he called it, the hellish looks of the Brownie interposed, and glued him to his seat.

"Hear what I have to say first," said the creature, "and then pore your fill on that precious book of yours. One concern at a time is enough. I came to do you a service. Here, take this cursed, wretched woman, whom you style your lady, and deliver her up to the lawful authorities, to be restored to her husband and her place in society. She is come upon one that hates her, and never said one kind word to her in his life, and though I have beat her like a dog, still she clings to me, and will not depart, so enchanted is she with the laudable purpose of cutting my throat. Tell your master and her brother, that I am not to be burdened with their maniac. I have scourged, I have spurned and kicked her, afflicting her night and day, and yet from my side she will not depart. Take her. Claim the reward in full, and your fortune is made, and so farewell."

The creature bowed and went away, but the moment his back was tyrned the lady fell a screaming and struggling like one in agony, and in spite of the old couple's exertions, she forced herself out of their hands, and ran after the retreating Merodach. When he saw better would not be, he turned upon her, and, by one blow with his stick, struck her down; and not content with that he continued to kick and baste her in such a manner as to all appearance would have killed twenty ordinary persons. The poor devoted dame could do nothing, but now and then utter a squeak like a half- worried cat, and writhe and grovel on the sward, till Wattie and his wife came up and withheld her tormentor from further violence. He then bound her hands behind her back with a strong cord, and delivered her once more to the charge of the old couple, who contrived to hold her by that means and take her home.

Wattie had not the face to take her into the hall, but into one of the outhouses, where he brought her brother to receive her. The man of the law was manifestly vexed at her reappearance, and scrupled not to testify his dissatisfaction; for when Wattie told him how the wretch had abused his sister, and that, had it not been for Bessie's interference and his own, the lady would have been killed outright,

"Why, Walter, it is a great pity that he did not kill her outright," said he. "What good can her life now do to her, or of what value is her life to any creature living? After one has lived to disgrace all connected with them, the sooner they are taken off the better."

The man, however, paid old Walter down his two thousand merks, a great fortune for one like him in those days: and not to dwell longer on this unnatural story, I shall only add, very shortly, that the Lady of Wheelhope soon made her escape once more, and flew, as by an irresistible charm, to her tormentor. Her friends looked no more after her: and the last time she was seen alive, it was following the uncouth creature up the water of Daur, weary, wounded, and lame, while he was all the way beating her, as a piece of excellent amusement. A few days after that, her body was found among some wild haggs, in a place called Crook-burn, by a party of the persecuted Covenanters that were in hiding there, some of the very men whom she had exerted herself to destroy, and who had been driven, like David of old, to pray for a curse and earthly punishment upon her. They buried her like a dog at the Yetts of Keppel, and rolled three huge stones upon her grave, which are lying there to this day. When they found her corpse, it was mangled and wounded in a most shocking manner, the fiendish creature having manifestly tormented her to death. He was never more seen or heard of in this kingdom, though all that country-side was kept in terror for him many years afterwards; and to this day, they will tell you of which title he seems to have acquired after his disappearance.

This story was told to me by an old man, named Adam Halliday, whose great grandfather, Thomas Halliday, was one of those that found the body and buried it. It is many years since I heard it: but, however ridiculous it may appear, I remember it made a dreadful impression on my young mind. I never heard any story like it, save one of an old foxhound that pursued a fox through the Grampians for a fortnight, and when at last discovered by the Duke of Athole's people, neither of them could run, but the hound was still continuing to walk after the fox, and when the latter lay down the other lay down beside him, and looked at him steadily all the while, though unable to do him the least harm. The passion of inveterate malice seems to have influenced these two exactly alike. But, upon the whole, I scarcely believe the tale can be true.

William Darby
(1775-1854)

Introduction
"Lydia Ashbaugh, the Witch"

This classic witch story is reprinted here for the first time since 1836. It is the sorrowful tale of how Lydia Ashbaugh became a witch and I hold it in high regard for its storyline and plot twists. "Lydia Ashbaugh" was originally published in the *Saturday Evening Post* and shortly thereafter in *Atkinson's Casket.* Both were Philadelphia concerns. The latter started publication in 1826. In December 1840, it was combined with *Burton's Gentleman's Magazine* by George Graham into *Graham's Magazine.* Edgar Allan Poe became its editor three months later.

The author of "Lydia Ashbaugh" is listed as Mark Bancroft, which is a pseudonym of William Darby (1775-1854), a member of the New York Historical Society and non-fiction historical author. Mark Bancroft is the name under which Darby wrote his fiction.

He confessed all in an April 18, 1834 autobiographical letter to family member, Dr. M. L. Dixon. "In 1829 I commenced supplying tales for "Atkinson's Casket," and have written all that species of writing which has appeared under the signature of Mark Bancroft. Recently I have made a regular engagement with Mr. Atkinson for a long series of border tales, ..."[5] Uniquely, Darby often made his pseudonym the protagonist in his stories and "Lydia Ashbaugh" is no exception. Though little is known about Darby today, he wrote a number of short Gothic romances that were published in the popular literary journals of his day: "The Vendue," "Clement Meyerfield and Clara

---

[5] William Darby, "Autobiographical Letter of William Darby," *Notes and Queries, Historical and Genealogical,* Ed. William Henry Engle, 1 (Harrisburg, Harrisburg Publishing Co., 1894), 39.

Ismeana,"[6] "Julia Gray, or the Orphan," "The Unknown,"[7] and "The Soldier's Tale."

Darby would be the most surprised of all to learn that he created one of the most remarkable witches of the first half of the 19th century. Her name is Lydia Ashbaugh.

Though Nathaniel Hawthorne's "The Hollow of the Hills" (1830) and "Young Goodman Brown" (1835) were published first, "Lydia Ashbaugh" is, in my view, America's first great witch story.

---

[6] Mark Bancroft, "Clement Meyerfield and Clara Ismeana," *The Casket*, 5 (May 1830), 205.

[7] Mark Bancroft, "The Unknown," *Atkinson's Casket*, 11:9 (September 1836), 434.

Lydia Ashbaugh, the Witch
1836

They remain these trifles to upbraid,
Out of the reach of spoil, and way of rage;
Though time with all his pow'r of years hath laid
Long batt'ry back'd with undermining age;
Yet they make head only with their own aid,
And war with his all conqu'ring forces wage;
Pleading the heaven's prescription to be free,
And t' have a grant t' endure as long as he.
DANIEL

THOUGH THE APPALACHIAN steeps do not rise to Alpine heights, nor, do they aspire to vie with the lowering Cordilleras, still they rise rock upon rock, wood crowned to awaken feelings of admiration and grandeur in the bosom which swells upon their rocky sides, or frowning brows. In infant years I gazed upon these fringed dells and beetling cliffs, and when more than half a century have past away, my heart warms with the remembrance. Oft since, have I revisited those mountains and oft have inwardly felt their immensity and unchangeableness–even their sterility seemed to mock the efforts of man, to give new features to works which rose with creation.

Rude and stern as are the lineaments of those children of ages, a smile sometimes breaks forth. In one of my rambling excursions I rose a mountain path but little frequented in the northern part of Franklin county, Pennsylvania. The day was an uncommonly clear and fine specimen of autumn. The air was bland and bracing, and at many openings of the forest I halted to gaze over the wide spread and farm decorated valley of Conedogwinat. As my narrow path merged into one of the public roads, a farm opened which fell partly down the mountain slope, and part opened on one of those fertile table lands so oft found along the Appalachian chains. Amid orchards, meadows, fields and gardens stood a stone house, which from the style of its architecture seemed anti-revolutionary, as did the barn and other out houses. The building stood in a mountain gap, from both sides of which fountains of purest limpid water gushed in abundant streams. It was and is a spot soft and beautiful amid scenes of grandeur, and from which spreads a landscape embracing much of Franklin and Cumberland counties, and far on the back ground rise the hills of Adams.

"How far to a public house?" I demanded of an old man I met opposite the Antique Mansion.

"Not far to a private one," he pleasantly replied, "but several miles to a tavern—but if it is rest and refreshment you want, walk in, this house is mine."

The manner of the patriarch and the allurements of the place were too seductive to be resisted and with some acknowledgements I entered. Dinner being ready, we sat down, and from my seat the view swept along the mountain slopes until lost in the far south western horizon. Amongst the crags of a not very distant precipice a white spot met my eye. It seemed too small and shapeless for a house and as my entertainer showed himself communicative, I asked him to explain the phenomena. At the question, the whole family, the old man, his wife and half dozen younger ones whom I afterwards found were their children, all exchanged looks with arch smiles. I sat rather confused until the old man seeing my embarrassment, apologised, and observed.—

"That is a house or rather our temple where we peep into futurity—in that house resides an old lady who can see farther into time than most people can into the north mountain."

I at once perceived that some joke lay beneath, and determined to give my share, replied "She might do that and not be able to tell who would be president of the United States in 1975."[8]

"Oh! Lydia Ashbaugh never consults her familiar on politics," subjoined the old man, "but a few of our young people and some of our old ones have learned their fortunes, and as mother Rarity, as she is an honest witch, tells often more than her inquirers like to hear."

"An honest witch," exclaimed I; "is a new character—I had thought the whole craft, honest or dishonest, had become extinct."

"You have just travelled far enough to find your mistake in the supernatural," replied mine host, "we have not only one but two species here in our back woods. Any of our girls who are young and beautiful, and more particularly if rich, they are witches."

Here for the soul of me I could not help exclaiming, "and more than one of that species are present"—as I glanced my eyes upon two of the most lovely and blushing faces that ever perched on an Appalachian giant.

"Yes," continued the not displeased parent, "but we have another species, not a jot more mischievous than the first, and in their way, as much sought after. When a woman is single, old, ugly, and of all things else, *poor*, she is a witch, and of these marks, mother Rarity possesses at least the three first, and the world gives her credit for the last, and the numbers are not small, who within ten miles of this spot most conscientiously believe that she can speak all languages, knows every thing, especially what is to be, and that she can be where she pleases, when she pleases."

Let none of the readers of the *Post*,[9] believe in their own infallibility so far as to suppose, that when they undertake to climb a mountain, they can leave human nature at the base; since, if I may decide this problem by my own

---

[8] Gerald Ford was president of the United States in 1975.

[9] Reference to the Philadelphia magazine the *Saturday Evening Post*, which was first published in 1821 and would later become one of America's largest circulating magazines.

example, I must confess I brought up all my share to the farm house, and consequently was seized with a most anxious desire to see a person answering so well to the witch of Endor; but concealing my wishes under an air of levity, I aided the merriment which went round at the expense of—But heavens, as we were in the midst of the mirth, the door was darkened and we all turned to see why, when to my sight appeared certainly the most extraordinary figure in the human form I had ever beheld.—The family seemed in no ways either surprised or alarmed, but I showed at least so much of the first that the apparition fixing her eyes, which were of powerful expression, on mine, observed—

"So Mark Bancroft is come to the north mountain to laugh at mother Rarity," and she grinned "a ghastly smile."

It may well be supposed this introduction did not lessen my expressions of astonishment, and my old host appeared to enjoy my confusion.

"Yes! old man," continued the hag, "well will it be around me, darkness was falling heavy over the deep for you if I don't change you into a rock or bear."

But I could perceive a lurking smile on the most expressive countenance I had ever beheld, and by the ill suppressed titter of the young, indeed the old ones, could easily see that the witch and the family understood each other, and all alike laughed under the ruse at the folly of some of their neighbours. This afforded me a clue which I was determined to pursue, and with a something of mock gravity begged pardon for my levity, and in turn, expressed my wonder how I could be known in a place so remote from my former walks.

"Oh! you are confounded," said the seer, "do you know that I was on the stone beside you when the old soldier related his tale?"

"Not the least suspicion crossed my mind that I was in such good company," replied I, "but since I have learned the fact, very much rejoiced am I."

"To have an emissary of the — and her master invisibly near you, eh!" interrupted mother Rarity, with a look which I too well remember even to forget, but which I shall not attempt to describe; it was just such a look as we might expect a witch to give to a person whom she knew to b e possessed of the true secret of her craft. — With this look and no farther ceremony, mother Rarity made a sign to my host which he no doubt understood as he rose, and apologising to me, observed he would return in a few moments, vanished into a back apartment of the house. The eyes of the residue of the family followed them with faces, as much as to say "we know."

Not quite as soon perhaps, as he himself expected, the old farmer and his terrible neighbour emerged again into view. The Emissary of the prince of the power of the air, as she issued from the council chamber, came close to me and in a half whisper observed, "mark, do you remember Marriott Cleveland," but not waiting an answer, glided out of the house, without turning her head, and with erect step was soon lost to my view amongst the orchard trees, over which a bye path led to her cottage. — I was riveted to the chair on which I was setting; my eyes followed the receding apparition, whilst a crowd of confused Recollections rushed on my mind. Things and persons long forgotten returned to memory, but with the incoherency of a dream. The family, who only heard the voice without distinguishing the words, all fixed their gaze on my abstracted countenance, with an inquiring scrutiny, but left me uninterrupted to reverie until some exciting thought roused me to the reflection, that I was on the blue mountain, and not on the banks of the Swatara, and awaking as if from a painful sleep, I looked around the room very much like a person who felt something abashed.

"Mother Rarity has touched you with her rod," at length observed the old farmer, smiling.

Very much relieved by a renewal of plain human conversation, I replied, "she has touched and taxed my memory not a little. How she has learned my name except by aid of her *old friend*, is more than my poor brain can divine, but let her knowledge come from once it may, she certainly does know my name, and of those I knew in my infant years more than my name." Here I paused, and indeed while speaking, came to a resolution which, however, I kept to myself, and rising, requested the charge for my fare.

The old farmer smiled and replied–"Nothing."

"Cheaper than city hospitality," rejoined I, "now favor me with the name of the mountain farmer who sets no value on the produce of his farm."

"Saul Standley does set great value on the produce of his farm, and when I can exchange it by cheering the sojourner, my price is paid." To this bowing I made a suitable reply and was again on my road.

The bland air, every moment changing mountain scenery, and the rather singular incidents of the day, all excited rapid reflections as I slowly descended the mountain. "I have not left Saul Standley's Hamlet to return no more, nor have I seen mother Rarity for the last time," muttered I to myself. "There have been some curious links in that part of the chain of my fortune which have been unwound, and no doubt these yet on the wheel are as variously twisted, contorted and rough to handle–indeed I must have a peep into the coil."

Indulging the judicious hope of having discovered a telescope with which to penetrate the distant and dark region of futurity and in scanning the delightful scenery around me, darkness was falling heavy over the deep veils before the thought came where I was to lay my head. Starting as from a dream, the landscape, late so resplendent, was shrouded in shades which every moment rendered more solemn. A dead silence gives a something of awful loneliness to my feelings. Suddenly I was arrested by the sharp barking of a small dog, who rushed almost to my feet, but retreating as I advanced, let me into a small opening of the woods in which appeared a cabin from which issued a man, who scolded his little noisy sentinel, then invited me to walk in.

"It is late friend" said I, "and necessary to find a lodging."

"Such as I have I am willing to give unto thee," replied the man, and ushered me into his cabin.

Here a scene opened to my view which with all I had before seen, was new. The man, much above the middle size, and under middle age, had at once the open countenance, yet something of stern, which those who are initiated can never mistake, and says to them very plainly, "this man has been an officer, and has seen service." Beside a table and cradle, sat all together the most striking female form I had ever beheld. Her face was not only pale but deadly pale, and yet her powerful black eyes seemed to have engrossed the whole energy of a soul of uncommon power. Her dress, as indeed everything in the cottage, was perfectly neat and clean; but the dress of this woman, in quality, bespoke coarseness and poverty, whilst in its adjustment and the easy air of the wearer appeared at being in disguise, a cultivated being who had been driven by adverse winds to this remote shelter.– While engaged in such common place conversation as rose from our mode of coming together, and while a full grown black man was setting our supper table, and while as far as politeness, perhaps further, would allow, I was examining around me, the lady, for lady she was, had drawn her nestling forth, just such a cherub a boy as might be expected as the child of such parents.

"Captain Woolford" at last observed the black servant, pointing to the supper table, And standing with the manner of a well drilled soldier when addressing his officer. a Frank welcome came rather from the countenances than from the words of my entertainers on whose faces, I could perceive an expression of sadness. After supper I was shown into a small shed room into a bed partaking of the general appearance of the house. The thin plank door permitted me to hear every word above a whisper, and though unwilling, I was compelled to be a listener to a conversation, which drew sleep from my eyelids, not only whilst it was carried on but for the residue of the night. my Scotch Irishified tone had led the unsuspecting husband and wife, no doubt into the belief that they could talk French in my hearing with impunity. While indeed spending the evening with these interesting people, I found something of foreign in the accents of the wife; I was now to find that she was in reality, though a native of Pennsylvania, a French woman by her mother, and a German by her father.

After my departure for some time, their words, those spoken with great energy, were inaudible, being spoken in tones little above a whisper, but as their minds became excited their voices were raised and assumed a painful earnestness.

"Oh my Caroline, my sweet little Frederic," at last burst from the man, "my own wretchedness is nothing–but the villain–"

"Cannot forever prosper," replied the wife–

"Prosper," interrupted the husband in bitterness, "yes! such is the world, he may prosper and we perish with our infant"–

Silence for a few moments followed this denunciation of the moral government of the world, but was broken by the man exclaiming "Caroline do you really think this man received your father's money?"

"As firmly as I believe my own being, and to the amount of at least twenty thousand dollars, and careless as my poor father was in his money affairs I have no doubt but that some written instrument was once in existence–but alas! that fire."

Hear the hard breathing of the man and the sobs of the woman, were the only sounds I heard from them for several minutes. she first regained her fortitude, and resumed observing–

"As to the claim which is crushing us, it is no doubt a forgery, but heaven will"–

"Yes! heaven has"–interrupted the man, and with this passionate exclamation, his words were again Followed by breathing almost convulsive, whilst his more reflecting wife continued in a tone which gradually calmed the husband.

"Oh! James why aggravate our situation by such language– have been preserved the on the battlefield–open thy noble breast and see that scar, which to my eye–yes! to my heart has always been the greatest beauty. Heaven gave thee life, reason, and integrity of soul above all wrong–If my unnatural uncle has robbed us, and if he drives us from this cabin, have we not health, education, and this," pointing no doubt to the face of their sleeping babe.

Never did I hear such an alteration of voice as I now heard from Captain James Wolford as he exclaimed, "God of infinite goodness and mercy forgive me, for thou knowest why I am tired–my own Caroline, my little Fred, my soul, my character, yes my utter contempt of all he can do."

There was evidently much of Camp religion in Captain Wolford's change of feeling, but with even that mixture, the change was salutary, and tranquilized the wife and mother, with much sweetness added.– "Glad indeed would I be to think that my–yes I'll say my wretched uncle, had as good cause to sleep soundly this night as we have."

Soon all was silent and peaceful round the rustic dwelling and I fully believed that the so recently distressed parents were wrapped in as profound forgetfulness of their misfortunes as were their sleeping boy, and my reflections on the mysterious ways of both guilt and innocence were at length interrupted, nor were they resumed until the increasing light of day roused me to a remembrance, that I was still an actor on a theatre where few knew the part they were soon to be compelled to act.

Habituated to early risings as I had been, my soldier host was up before me; and as I issued from the bed room was met by a man on whose face no despondency appeared–in the contrary, the first smile I had seen to unbend his features, beamed on me as he observed, "my friend you are not a prisoner of war but of peace, and cannot be discharged until after breakfast."

"Your commands must be obeyed," Captain Woolford, I replied–"such captivity is not very distressing–and if it had the burthen, would have been removed by the entrance of the angel of the scene."

What means I should have adopted to obtain more insight into the peculiar cause of distress so imperfectly revealed the evening before I know not, as plans have been laid in my breast previously to remain in the vicinity some time, and of course, expected to receive what I desired from public gossip. Our meal completed, with such acknowledgments only which such people would receive, I departed.

Still early and in the deep mountain valley the sun's light came only by reflection, and the long shadows of one ridge fell with a solemn and every moment changeful effect on its western neighbor. My path led me under a projecting precipice, rendered more gloomy by a brow of cedars and thick underwood. Glimpses of numerous farms flashed amongst the branches and foliage at intervals, and I was thinking to myself how I should proceed to obtain quarters for a few weeks, when my cogitations were completely interrupted by a figure gliding as if issuing from the bosom of the mountain, and mother Rarity stood before me. How long we stood staring at each other I know not. My feelings were those of unutterable surprise. The countenance of the woman, I remember strongly but shall admit the vein attempt at description; there was an expression of mischief and derision. Whether or not she was awaiting me to break silence, I had not sufficient reflection to determine, but with a curl of lip which might indeed well have suited a witch, she roused me to something like common sense by observing "Mark Bancroft bewitched," and laughed, such a laugh–it was not loud but awful, but as her features regained composure I with a little of embarrassment replied, "good woman would you ought with me?"

"Good woman, alas!" she inwardly murmured, and remaining silent for some time; abstracted, as if some terrible recollection had risen, and as I stood the image of astonishment at the strange rencounter with a being who it was evident knew my name, but of whom with every effort of memory I could recall no trace.

"Yes!" at length she replied in great earnestness of manner, "I have sought thee for a purpose which will speak to thy soul. When thou departed yesterday from the door of one of the best men in whose house now has ever entered,

I followed thee, and saw thee entering the house of mourning, but"–and here again she paused, whilst I remained in mute and really painful suspense to learn to what the scene was to lead.

"I saw thee enter," at length she resumed, "the Mansion of sorrow, and now invite thee to the witch's cave." Before I could answer she beckoned, and following her round the projecting rocks and by means of the scattered shrubs some distance up the mountain, until our view over topped the trees of the valley below, and we had reached a shelf from which a most delightful landscape spread far down the mountain vale. Raising her shriveled right arm and pointing to a very large farm house, observed in a voice which thrilled to my heart.

"Yesterday thou satest at the board of innocence and worth, today–for why I am bound, but not now to explain, thou must enter the doors of hardened villainy, but"–and her gritted teeth and face displayed a ferocity, I never could have thought was human. The paroxysm was, however, brief, and she resumed.

"Amuse myself until the sun has commenced a downward course, and then approach, enter and seek refreshment in that house. Thy money will procure what nature demands, observe the master of the house, scan his features, and then think if you ever before seen such–turn Vine eye up the mountain side to the left. Mark that white spot; it is a cabin passed by a path. Follow that path over the mountain top. Then turn your view to the left again and you will see a dark roof.–it is the cave of mother Rarity, but enter it not with day light."–so saying she whirled round with the rapidity of a bird, while, "fail not" was the last words I heard from her shriveled and compressed lips as darting round a projection of the rocky ledge, she disappeared.

"Strange! strange!" muttered I to myself "that I should be spellbound by such a being, but I am, and must know why, and as if compelled by in irresistible power, followed her directions. The day was sultry and close for autumn weather, and fatigued with rambles some time after midday, I entered the house so terribly denounced by the mysterious woman. I was indeed met at the threshold by those harbingers of inhospitality, two fierce dogs, which were, however, silenced by a man of middle-age who advanced, and when the noise of his sentinels were hushed, demanded my business in no inviting tone.

"My business," I replied, "is to procure a dinner for which I expect to pay"–Umph, was the reply as he waved me in with a sweep of his brawny hand and arm–it is probable had no intimation been given of the man, I should have regarded his physiognomy in a high degree sinister, but influenced as I felt the glance of his dark and deep set eyes excited almost a shutter. He was taciturn and replied to my remarks by monosyllables, and to my few questions still more briefly. But he could not prevent nor suspect the true object of my visit, which in fact, I very faintly surmised myself. My dinner, which was coarse, being finished and paid for, I departed and as directed, ascended the mountain, ever and anon halting to behold the fine, and every moment changing, scenery, and ruminating on the singular lodging house I was approaching–but slow as I advanced, the afternoon seemed to lengthen as my curiosity became more intense, and the long shadows of evening appeared to linger as if to mock my impatience. Before the sun had sunk behind the western mountains, I found myself seated on a rock amid a grove of chestnut saplings, above the cottage of the witch. As twilight fell black and heavy, the unbroken silence was awful. A storm would have given relief, but not a leaf moved, not a sound disturbed the fearful pause. As the moments of entering the loan habitation at length came round, I must confess the palace of an emperor would have been approached with less trepidation. *But what must be must be*, thought I, as a hand cold and hard touched my cheek. Starting to my feet, in the gloom of the now closing night, stood before me a form which could not be mistaken–it was the witch.

"Enter and fear not," was her invitation as she turned and led me into the cave, for such in part was her dwelling.

A lamp shedding faint light over bare walls–walls of rough hewn and unwashed logs. Combined with the circumstances which preceded, there was a chilling horror in the scene. Before me stood the tall form of the recluse, her hollow visage and gray locks bespeaking pain and sorrow. Mute we stood for a few moments, when in a totally changed voice she earnestly exclaimed:

"Lord I think thee," and turning around flung open a door and to my utter surprise, on a table covered with green cloth stood two elegant silver candlesticks, with two brilliant candles shedding strong light over a white washed room. This room was without regular form as it was partly excavated from the natural rock. A bed stood on one side and clothing covered with dust hung on the walls, as did several picture frames, screened with black gauze, also rendered gray with dust. A large Bible and several other books lay on the table. Opposite to the bed stood a bookcase, which from the workmanship was evidently a relic of a past century, but now appeared as if formed by an electric stroke, standing as if shattered by some explosive force.

"Look around," said the woman, "you are now in a room no human being but myself has ever before entered. It was formed by him, who also formed these mountains, and fashioned by these hands; quote and she held up her long, bony, slender, and grounded and sinewy arms and hands before my face.

I could bear in silence the scene no longer, and with something of irritation, observed, "Woman why all this? for what am *I* here?"

Her lips quivered but her looks quelled not as she steadfastly returned my fixed look, and replied by repeating, "for what am I here?" having energetic emphasis on I; and turning round while her eyes were still fixed on mine, she removed the veil from before one of the pictures. The moment the crape was removed I started back, exclaiming with the utmost astonishment, "Sophia Markland." Before me appeared a half length portrait of a well-known face, but a face I had not seen for nearly thirty years; but the fine blue eyes, exquisite teint and expression, the glossy and abundant ringlets, and a thousand painful remembrances, all rushed upon my heart with electric rapidity. My hostess left me a few moments a victim to surprise indescribable, until I again half inwardly murmured, "poor murdered sophia, where did heaven's vengeance sleep when thy betrayer and Destroyer escaped?"

"Heaven's never slept," interrupted the woman, "but like the spark which sifted that casket," pointing to the shattered desk, "the stroke may be delayed." She again paused and then continued, "what dost thou suppose was the final fate of Sophia markland?"

"Drowned in the Susquehanna, alas!" I replied.

"In which her corpse was never found," rejoined the woman.

"Not that I ever learned"–

"Or could learn," was the rapid interruption, "years of tears, pain, sickness, remorse, and all else, which can render life a punishment, would have been saved to the miserable Sophia, had the water been her friend as supposed. But Mark bancroft, time presses–we cannot wait to trifle–turn your eyes from the unconscious picture and look on this face."

I did turn, and scanned the wrinkled features in vain to surmise why the request.

"The ruin is too complete," she at length exclaimed in bitterness, "not of Sophia Markland," and she sunk into a chair, her head falling between her knees, with convulsive sobs–

A flash of lighting seemed to pass over my mind, and in its glare appeared the spirit of the long lost Sophia. I paced the room for some time at intervals repeating the name, and that of Eltham Heathfield,–names too fearfully connected. I was now convinced that the wasted and withered form beside me, was what remained of the once most attractive and beautiful Sophia, but I suffered the storm of regret to spend its force and then, drawing a chair, sat down beside the recluse, and in a soothing tone observed, "Sophia, for you are Sophia, remember the days of our youth." My words fell as balm on a wounded heart, and raising her head, she smiled as a sun beam from a summer cloud, and ejaculated–"Oh how delightful twenty-five long years have passed since the human voice has fallen on this heart in kindness."

She Rose and passing into the outer room, bathed her feverish head with cool water, returned and sat down with a composure as if nothing extraordinary had occurred, but her eye falling perhaps accidentally, on the representation of what she had been, she started up, replace the veil and again sat down, and pulling out a drawer of the table, drew forth a bundle of papers, bound with a blue ribbon, laid them between us with the mysterious observation, "*heaven's vengeance reposes but sleeps not in that packet,*" and then continued. "I am now to explain, why we are both here? therefore hear the witch's story.–Fear no listeners. Those who are above the belief of witches, are above the meanness, and those who are not, would expect worse than the vengeance of heaven if they dared come near this cell in stealth."

"The history of my family I need not relate–all that is known to thee as well as to myself–nor need I recall the too much courted Sophia, but it is necessary I should relate circumstances, with which you were, with the world in general, only acquainted by common report. While in Philadelphia, completing my education, I was accidentally introduced to a young man, whose name, Eltham Heathfield, will be ere long restored to your recollection. At the moment, considered beautiful, and greatly richer than I was, in fact, flattered, followed, envied and hated by most of my female *friends*, and pursued as prey by some of the other sex. Passions too powerful for reason, but with a heart in which neither affections nor its opposite were moderate, it was not in my power to love otherwise than to excess. To most of the young gentlemen of my circle, I was merely acquainted by sight to most of them, my feelings at least were those of indifference. To all this, Eltham Heathfield was an exception. Mixing with the first society, his manners were polished–his coldness I then attributed to good sense–but I was to learn a deeper cause. A near relation of the family in which I boarded, he felt he had unlimited admittance to my company and he profited from the advantage. Few words now are left–I was deeply, purely, and unchangeably as I thought, attached, and in the full confidence of full return was in the warmth of youth, planning how faithfully the duties of wife should be performed. No reason have I now to disguise it and in the face of heaven I declare, I do not believe any other woman ever more sincerely looked forward to wedded happiness founded on faithful discharge of the highest applications.

These were dreams–youthful dreams–my guardian spirit slept and I became the slave of a powerful villain. My idol was changed to a demon. The visits of my destroyer were made at lengthening intervals–still, however, though rendered less happy, I was unconscious of the gulf opening before me. Seated one evening on a sofa in the common parlor–the sun had set, but the candles not yet lighted, I felt something of undefined distress, from which I was roused by a well-known dread.–The figure glided in and without speaking presented a letter which in the dim light I could but see, and also in silence, wheeled out, and in much astonishment I was again alone. "This is a new freak of Eltham," thought I, as ringing for a light, I rose and when the light came, went up stairs to my own room. With an anxiety I could not repress or account, for the letter was opened, and with an effort yet to me inscrutable, it was red and thrown on the table. My very soul felt frozen. The whole horrors of my situation lay before me, painted in few words by my murderer–for all for to all purposes of earthly enjoyment, death spread his veil over me from that fatal night,–a night on which no bed was pressed by the ruined Sophia. But everyone has their own manner of meeting calamity. Happiness and the man who trampled on my heart were gone together–that heart was bruised, but not crushed–love was there replaced by hatred–undying hatred."– And there she paused and all the demons shook her frame and distorted her truly haggard features–but the storm had a pause and she resumed.

"Over a fallen daughter there was no mother to weep, and wither brokenhearted–no sister to share the blight of lost reputation–no brother to pierce or be pierced by the foul betrayer–but there was a father, gray with age, and feeble and health to receive or reject an airing child.–To that father, I was determined to appeal–on earth he was the only hope, and failed me not in the hour of shame and sorrow. To my native home I fled, leaving my city friends to their surmises. On my father's breast I learned, and to his heart was taken, forgiven and consoled, as far as human consolation would soften misery like mine. In the very room where I was born, I became the mother of a son, whom erst I had hoped to bestow on a doting husband and father.

"Utterly secluded, and seen only by my only parent, and a deaf and dumb servant girl, I nursed my babe, watering his innocent face with my tears. My father, you know, was a man of uncommon good sense, and I know he was also a man of kindness and feeling, and why he sunk not to the grave under so much affliction from the hand of an only daughter, is all together unaccountable, but he is still living, and with all the world but yourself, believes the tale of my suicide in the Susquehanna. In open day my native farm is visible from this den. But I must haste to conclude my story of wretchedness.

"The name of my seducer was never repeated to my father–indeed the only stern command I ever received from him was not to name the monster–a command I had no inclination to disobey. Time passed and my boy began to lisp in our native tongue, when, as was his daily custom, my father came in and sitting down began to play with little James, observing "we have a new neighbor, Thomas Milford has sold his farm to a newcomer named Eltham Heathfield," and diverted by the child's gambols, the effect on me was unobserved. In fact my heart was frozen to every thing beyond the room, but even he must yield. The cruelty that had been practiced upon me now came home more terribly than ever. No exertion of mind would prevent me from contrasting what I might,–what I ought to be as the mistress of the very farm on which you paid for a miserable dinner this day–yes! that sour miser–that suffering wretch, poor in possession of great wealth, is Eltham Heathfield.

"Knowledge of his existing in our vicinity prayed upon me–I became a fretful, irritable, and disrespectful to my protector, my father, and only friend. The face of my boy became even hateful–I thought I could trace a likeness which a disordered mind rendered striking. My father noticed, and attributed my altered conduct to sickness, but it was not sickness of body; it was worse; it was sickness of mind. At some moments I was conscious of my true situation, but in solitude, the brain was prayed upon by the horrid phantoms of its own creation."

Here she paused and sat as if listening to some distant voice–but it was the effect of overpowering remembrance, and as I sat the picture of anxious attention, she started and resumed.

"You are now to hear what will require all your confidence to believe possible. As the sun shown through a grated window, I awoke, and starting up to call my child, which I thought in the bed–no child was there. I then called to my father–the walls answered by echo. I stared around me, everything was changed. Springing to my feet, I stood petrified and exclaimed, "this must be a dream," and to convince myself I was not dreaming, actually struck the wall with my forehead. I was no longer deceived, but reason would soon again have deserted its post, had not a door opened and a woman, an entire stranger, but with a most benevolent look, stood before me. I was motionless with an utterable wonder, as she advanced toward me, taking my hand and leading me back to the bed, "am I in the regions of the dead?" I at length demanded.

"'Poor sufferer,' replied my protector, 'you are still amongst the children of mortality–you are on earth–but lie down and be composed.' I obeyed and she sat down by me, and in a most mild and tender tone I was comforted.

"My reason was restored–but many days elapsed before I learned that I had been five years in a mad house, in the state of ________ four hundred miles from my home. The first time I beheld myself in a mirror, I started back with horror. I could not have believed that death itself could have made such a change. my hair was now scanty and gray–all the most fearful ravages of age and distress were united. I requested a Bible and one was given to me. I read, reflected, and found that my intellects were restored, and then requested the presence of the attending physician. He came, and in him I met a gentleman, and a man of real science on the subject he was appointed to superintend. In a few conversations he became convinced of my sanity. With the cunning of madness, I had concealed my name, and though I made the physician a confident so far as to account for my recent situation, my name, place of birth or any circumstance which could lead to any knowledge of myself or connections, I concealed.

"Dead I am regarded, no doubt, by all whoever knew me." I inwardly reflected, "and that I am determined to remain–no one can recognize Sophia Markland under this disguise. tenderly–in reality, too tenderly nurtured, I was very unprepared to labor for a living, but I was determined to labor. Silent, submissive, and regarded as a repentant Magdalene, I found many compassionate hearts. How or by what possible means I had wandered over the space between the insane hospital and my native home, I never can know, as I never can remember; but over the same space I returned as a common female laborer, and still a young woman in years but blasted by misfortune. I recrossed the Susquehanna, and again beheld my native mountains, perfect mistress of my mother's language, the German; I assumed the name by which, when I am not known as mother Rarity, I have since passed. Performing the duty of a common servant, Lydia Ashbaugh has remained unsuspected in her own father's house–has attended in sickness and health, her own son, and wept over him bitter tears which fell unseen by mortal eye. In several instances my own tragic story has been related to me or in my hearing, with all its additions of falsity. Some of my clothing was found according to the tale, on an island near Harrisburg, but my body by report, to have been found. Not a living soul out of this room, I sincerely believe, has the most distant suspicion that Lydia Ashbaugh is the ruin of Sophia Markland, and to my grave should the secret have descended, had not recent circumstances opened a scene which compels me to unmask, to save my son from the fangs. but let me be cool."–cool as far as passion could excite heat, she was not–but as before, I let the fire burn, and after another pause she again continued.

"Determined that my child should not, as far as I could prevent it, share his mother's shame and wretchedness, I stopped frequenting   my father's house as James approached manhood. This ground on which I reside was the property of my mother, and is of course now mine; I have actually leased it from my own father. First, a ridiculous story was raised by ignorance that I was a witch, or worse. I had long ceased to laugh, but I smiled at the notion of supernatural association, and finding it through an atmosphere of fear around me, I let it pass. The wise laugh and the fools dread, and so let them. The hour is hasting on when my real power will be shown in thunder."

"Amid all my trials and changes, from the moment I received the fatal letter from the hand of Eltham Heathfield, there is one passion which has never abated in my bosom. a voice always seemed to whisper, "the day will come when you can take vengeance on that man." This voice I have heard in whispers In all hours of the day and night, in every season of the year; on the return of long suspended reason, it came again and animated me in toil. In search of this, a good twenty-five years have I toiled, and am now very soon to reap the fruits, and astonishing as it may sound in your ears, in part by your aid–interrupt me not –you will soon hear and gladly will your aid be granted. But let me return back on time.

"Maria Heathfield, once the sister of an unworthy brother, was much the younger of the two they were the only children of parents long departed, and to rid himself probably of superintending her education, Maria was sent to in aunt in Philadelphia, where at an age too little advanced to admit much reflection, she fell into company with an immigrant French gentlemen, which eventuated into attachment and marriage. In many respects Maria was fortunate in her connections. M. Steven Montault, was a gentleman in the proper meaning of the term. He was tender and affectionate to his wife, and transported with delight when they're only child, a daughter, called Caroline, bloomed in sportiveness. Montault was for this country, rich, but remarkably confiding. This quality was cultivated to profit by Heathfield the brother, who in a very few years had contrived to borrow most of his brother-in-law's capital. but matters went smooth on the surface until the declining health and final death of Maria removed the tie between them.

"Rendered wretched by the loss of his adored wife and becoming dissatisfied with the conduct of her brother, Montault demanded the return of his money, announcing his intention to remove to New York. Difficulties increased, and from a real friendship on the part of the Frenchman, open enmity succeeded, and legal redress was threatened. Things were in this train, when in the dead of night the house of Montault was involved in flames.–The fire I believe was accidental, but his character exposed Heathfield to suspicion. The natural impulse of Montault in the alarm was to save his child, which he affected with great difficulty, and at the expense of his own life, scorched by the flames. A raging fever was the consequence, and from the moment of seeing his child in safety, Steven Montault never was in a situation to give any direction as to his affairs, and on the sixth day after his last misfortune, was laid beside the remains of his wife.

"Now all was changed with his family; Maria was an orphan, at the mercy of her unnatural uncle. He administered the property, sold in due time the personal effects, and no doubt to blind the world, sent Caroline to Philadelphia, where, whatever was his motive, she received her education. A few things were saved from the fire, and amongst the rest, that desk, which after falling into other hands was sold to me for a trifle–but little indeed did I suspect its value. In that corner it stood many years, while other changes were in the womb of time. I never committed a theft but one, if that was really a theft–I stole my own picture and placed it over the desk, and there have they dust-covered remained, shut from every eye but mine.

"While all these events were occurring, my son rose to manhood. The idol of my poor old father, James, received a tolerable education. In a mother's eye he was not only a fine, but an elegant young man, and little did he suppose that the heart of a fond mother beat in the bosom of the menial that took her highest pleasure in washing and arranging his clothing. Mystery indeed hung over his birth, though under the name of James Wolford, start not– Captain James Wolford is my son, and Caroline was once Caroline Montault; but be calm and listen. The last war called to the field many others, and amongst them my noble boy. Oh! how my bosom beat when honored with wounds and high in character, he returned into his native country. The train of circumstances which brought James and Caroline together, you will learn at a future day; suffice it to say that to my delight they became man and wife, but their uncle neither felt nor pretended to feel great indignation, and whatever was the motive, his enmity was durable and serious. The long minority of Caroline left her uncle undisturbed, and when her husband made demands on her property, they were met by the taunt that they had nothing to receive, but on the contrary a large claim against her father was urged. My son was irritated at what he regarded injustice, and unconscious of their real relationship, personal violence was only prevented by the interference of others. After the most diligent search, not a trace of ligation could be found to substantiate the rights of Caroline to her father's property. Involved in lawsuits and persecuted by a haughty relation, this father and mother are now reduced to indigence, and despair; but how will their condition be changed tomorrow!"

Now beamed something of the once beautiful Sophia Markland. She Rose to her feet–her eye shot with a lustre, I could not behold without astonishment; but she checked her transports and again sat down, seizing at the same time the packet which during her harrowing narrative lay on the table. "You see that broken desk," said she pointing to the ruined peace. "It shall be mended with clasps of silver."

If I was riveted by any part of the scene, I was still more so at what was now placed before me. With great composure Sophia unfolded the papers, and laid them on the table writing downwards–when done, she again addressed me in words not to be forgotten.

"You remember the thunderstorm of last week," "well" I replied–" and well do I remember it," she subjoined, "never subject to dread lightning and thunder, on the contrary, from a child I was rather delighted with the awful display, and on the night I have mentioned, I was sitting in that outer room viewing the flashes and hearing the echoes from mountain to mountain, when I was stunned by an explosion which seemed to burst from the earth and rent her bowels. My desolate dwelling was struck–you see that split beam. From that the shock fell upon the desk, and threw the fragments over the room. A remark I had once heard in Philadelphia now occurred to my mind. "It was that the same place or same object is never, or very rarely, if ever, affected twice by the electricity of the same storm, and that any object or place once touched by an electric shock, is really never again subject to like accident. I therefore now regarded my cabin in safety, and as the storm passed away sought my lone couch, and with the elements was soon at rest.

"The next morning as they strengthened, I saw the effect of the stroke of the bolt. The desk was literally severed, but those and some other papers arrested my attention, and on examination I found that the back part had contained a secret till or kind of drawer, which burst by the explosion, its contents lay scattered over the floor. After examining some loose fragments of no moment, I picked up the one containing these papers; and now let us glance upon their faces, and learn what they reveal, and here do you know that writing?" saying this she handed me the paper, and what was my astonishment to see a document written in a hand of great neatness and peculiarity, it was that of a teacher, under whose care I had myself learned to write–but of infinitely greater importance was its tenor. It was a duly executed mortgage, for the money lent by Steven Montault to his brother-in-law, and the other documents in the same packet were bonds and other obligations which had been thus far remarkably preserved.

"In mingled joy and astonishment, I read these precious records, handing them over to the exalting mother, who again folding them up very carefully while observing, "on to-morrow a meeting is to take place at Saul Standley's– who is not only justice of the peace, but a peacemaker. Eltham Heathfield is to meet his injured son.–He shall have chance more to recede and do justice. Let him refuse and all shall be revealed–If, but I need not hope, his day is come, and my son and his wife and child shall be restored to their rights. You can attest to this hand writing come what will. Be at Standley's and before midday tomorrow.

The reader need not be told that I was at Standley's at the time appointed, and found by the manner of the old squire that I was expected. I was first on the ground but had not long to wait. Captain James Wolford was next. His noble countenance was care worn, and I could, or thought I could, see despair and anxiety contending, and dreaded the consequence on his mind of the revelation I knew was to be made. My lips were, however, sealed. The last words of Sophia Markland, to me on partying, were "let Heathfield do justice, and then what has passed must forever remain unknown to the world."

The distressed Wolford was too much occupied with his forebodings of evil to speak much, and I for a different reason was also silent, but watched with increasing anxiety the path over the field where I knew the witch would approach. Her figure at length appeared, and when at some distance Wolford observed her, and exclaimed "Good God is that woman to be here."

I could not refrain from observing, "that woman will do you know harm." Wolford regarded me in silent displeasure, and conscious of my own imprudence, I felt too awkward to give excuse, nor really had I time, as Sophia entered, and to the surprise of the family, well and neatly dressed, and was quickly followed by Heathfield.

"What a meeting between a father and son, " said I, mentally. A scowl of the most repulsive kind sat on the face of the father, and to the friendly greeting of the old magistrate he scarcely deemed to grumble a reply, and without sitting down, very roughly demanded, "what is the particular object of troubling me to come here, squire?" and without allowing the squire to explain, went on, "I was not obliged to come, nor have I much time to wait."

Every eye in the room was fixed on him, but there was one of intense scrutiny, and which as he closed his rude address to the magistrate drew his full attention, as the question met his ear. "Elpham Heathfield, do you intend to do justice to your brother's child?" he evidently shrunk from the speaker, but attempted to conceal his feelings by turning to the squire and asking in a loud tone, "What has this hag to do with my affairs?" This fatal expression sealed his fate. Sophia had entered the house with her portrait carefully wrapped up, and as the insulting term hag fell from Heathfield, she laid the frame on the table as she rose. Her form always commanding, seemed to gain supernatural height. "Hag," she repeated as Heathfield quailed under her dreadful glance, "and are you prepared to learn who made me a hag?–Do you dare to look on that face?" and she unwrapped her portrait and sat it before him, the very heart's blood of the man seemed frozen–his face assumed a hue incomparably more appalling than death. Every joint shook, and his tongue cleaved to the roof of his mouth–not so Sophia, who with an expression of ineffable disdain again repeated "hag–yes! in madness, in sickness, in shame and in poverty, and even in what have I been for long and bitter years a hag, the scorn of the base and an object of pity to the good–long have I awaited this hour and now I hurl back on the head of my betrayer, the obloquy he has heaped on mine–once more Heathfield, are you ready to do justice to your brother's daughter?" What answer the crushed and confounded wretch would have made can never be known, as while his lips quivered, she was too much excited to wait and in a voice of still more dreadful import added, "No! under any circumstance can you do justice, but justice shall be done on you–behold that man and she pointed to Wolford, who with us all stood without the power of words or motion, awaiting the termination of a scene in which so many developments seemed to rise as from the grave.

"Do you examine that face carefully, while I prepare something more for your comfort." The faces indeed of the father and son, for very different reasons were indeed steadfastly fixed on each other, as Sophia laying down her portrait, opened the packet, handing one paper after another to the old and astonished magistrate, and then again addressing Heathfield, observed. "A few fleeting moments and you might have retired to your home, and so would I have gone to mine, and went to the grave unrevenged–for as the hour approached I shrunk from revealing to that injured man who was his father. But–but– I could not see him and his wife and child robbed. Behold your son and mine!

In a moment the mother and son were in each other's arms. the father heard no more–he fell writhing in agony, and–but let me draw a veil over the residue of this scene.

   *   *   *   *   *   *   *   *

*

In a few days after the funeral of the uncle, Maria Woolford, for his mother and grandfather would not hear of his assuming the name of Heathfield, and her husband therefore was by her made master of the ample fortune of his father. The mother removed and resided with them, but remains secluded with very great caution. Her existence was made known to her aged father, who in a few years breathed his last breath upon her bosom. In memory of their many visitors and in the calm enjoyments of the goods of the earth, this family lives in tranquility and peace. The very name of Heathfield is a forbidden sound in their dwelling.

Nathaniel Hawthorne
(1804-1864)

Introduction
"Young Goodman Brown"

Hawthorne's second witch tale, "Young Goodman Brown," is arguably his most popular short story. It was originally published in Boston's *The New England Magazine* in the April 1835 issue. The story was simply credited to "the author of 'The Gray Champion.'" This was in reference to the short story that appeared in Hawthorne's *Twice Told Tales*. "Young Goodman Brown," was subsequently collected in Hawthorne's anthology *Moses from an Old Manse* in 1846. It is filled with underlying meaning, just as many of Hawthorne's popular novels like *The House of Seven Gables* and *The Scarlet Letter*. One need look no further than the *double entendre* of "Faith," the name of Goodman Brown's wife. At the beginning of the story he is presented with the moral choice of staying with Faith or venturing into the world, which in this case happens to be a foreboding and dark woods. It is a place where the devil and witches await.

Sadly, "Young Goodman Brown," trips all over itself with allegory, causing what could have been a better story to stumble its way across the pages. Hawthorne never shied away from teaching morals through symbolism. "Young Goodman Brown" is no exception. Herman Melville thought it was "as deep as Dante." Henry James, perhaps with tongue in cheek, called it a "magnificent little romance."

Debate about this little witch tale shows no signs of stopping. When compared to Hawthorne's "The Hollow of the Three Hills," "Young Goodman Brown" has proved the more popular witch story perhaps due it receiving much scholarly attention. This is a result of its pervasive allegory throughout.

Yet, when allegory gets in the way of the story, it needs to be rooted out. As a result, in my view, Earnest Theodore Hoffmann's novella "The First of May, or Wallburga's Night" and Nikolai Gogol's "Viy" are much better examples of witches run amok in the early part of the 19th century.

Young Goodman Brown
1835

YOUNG GOODMAN BROWN came forth at sunset into the street at Salem village; but put his head back, after crossing the threshold, to exchange a parting kiss with his young wife. And Faith, as the wife was aptly named, thrust her own pretty head into the street, letting the wind play with the pink ribbons of her cap while she called to Goodman Brown.

"Dearest heart," whispered she, softly, and rather sadly, when her lips were close to his ear, "prithee put off your journey until sunrise and sleep in your own bed tonight. A lone woman is troubled with such dreams and such thoughts that she's afeard of herself sometimes. Pray tarry with me this night, dear husband, of all nights in the year."

"My love and my Faith," replied young Goodman Brown, "of all nights in the year, this one night must I tarry away from thee. My journey, as thou callest it, forth and back again, must needs be done 'twixt now and sunrise. What, my sweet, pretty wife, dost thou doubt me already, and we but three months married?”

“Then God bless you!” said Faith, with the pink ribbons; “And may you find all well when you come back.”

“Amen!” cried Goodman Brown. “Say thy prayers, dear Faith, and go to bed at dusk, and no harm will come to thee.”

So they parted; and the young man pursued his way until, being about to turn the corner by the meeting-house, he looked back and saw the head of Faith still peeping after him with a melancholy air, in spite of her pink ribbons.

“Poor little Faith!” thought he, for his heart smote him. “What a wretch am I to leave her on such an errand! She talks of dreams, too. Methought as she spoke there was trouble in her face, as if a dream had warned her what work is to be done tonight. But no, no; ’twould kill her to think it. Well, she’s a blessed angel on earth; and after this one night I’ll cling to her skirts and follow her to heaven.”

With this excellent resolve for the future, Goodman Brown felt himself justified in making more haste on his present evil purpose. He had taken a dreary road, darkened by all the gloomiest trees of the forest, which barely stood aside to let the narrow path creep through, and closed immediately behind. It was all as lonely as could be; and there is this peculiarity in such a solitude, that the traveler knows not who may be concealed by the innumerable trunks and the thick boughs overhead; so that with lonely footsteps he may yet be passing through an unseen multitude.

“There may be a devilish Indian behind every tree,” said Goodman Brown to himself; and he glanced fearfully behind him as he added, “What if the devil himself should be at my very elbow!”

His head being turned back, he passed a crook of the road, and, looking forward again, beheld the figure of a man, in grave and decent attire, seated at the foot of an old tree. He arose at Goodman Brown’s approach and walked onward side by side with him.

“You are late, Goodman Brown,” said he. “The clock of the Old South was striking as I came through Boston, and that is full fifteen minutes agone.”

“Faith kept me back a while,” replied the young man, with a tremor in his voice, caused by the sudden appearance of his companion, though not wholly unexpected.

It was now deep dusk in the forest, and deepest in that part of it where these two were journeying. As nearly as could be discerned, the second traveler was about fifty years old, apparently in the same rank of life as Goodman Brown, and bearing a considerable resemblance to him, though perhaps more in expression than features. Still they might have been taken for father and son. And yet, though the elder person was as simply clad as the younger, and as simple in manner too, he had an indescribable air of one who knew the world, and who would not have felt abashed at the governor's dinner table or in King William's court, were it possible that his affairs should call him thither. But the only thing about him that could be fixed upon as remarkable was his staff, which bore the likeness of a great black snake, so curiously wrought that it might almost be seen to twist and wriggle itself like a living serpent. This, of course, must have been an ocular deception, assisted by the uncertain light.

"Come, Goodman Brown," cried his fellow-traveler, "this is a dull pace for the beginning of a journey. Take my staff, if you are so soon weary."

"Friend," said the other, exchanging his slow pace for a full stop, "having kept covenant by meeting thee here, it is my purpose now to return whence I came. I have scruples touching the matter thou wot'st of."

"Sayest thou so?" replied he of the serpent, smiling apart. "Let us walk on, nevertheless, reasoning as we go; and if I convince thee not thou shalt turn back. We are but a little way in the forest yet."

"Too far! too far!" exclaimed the goodman, unconsciously resuming his walk. "My father never went into the woods on such an errand, nor his father before him. We have been a race of honest men and good Christians since the days of the martyrs; and shall I be the first of the name of Brown that ever took this path and kept—"

"Such company, thou wouldst say," observed the elder person, interpreting his pause. "Well said, Goodman Brown! I have been as well acquainted with your family as with ever a one among the Puritans; and that's no trifle to say. I helped your grandfather, the constable, when he lashed the Quaker woman so smartly through the streets of Salem; and it was I that brought your father a pitch-pine knot, kindled at my own hearth, to set fire to an Indian village, in King Philip's War. They were my good friends, both; and many a pleasant walk have we had along this path, and returned merrily after midnight. I would fain be friends with you for their sake."

"If it be as thou sayest," replied Goodman Brown, "I marvel they never spoke of these matters; or, verily, I marvel not, seeing that the least rumor of the sort would have driven them from New England. We are a people of prayer, and good works to boot, and abide no such wickedness."

"Wickedness or not," said the traveler with the twisted staff, "I have a very general acquaintance here in New England. The deacons of many a church have drunk the communion wine with me; the selectmen of divers towns make me their chairman; and a majority of the Great and General Court are firm supporters of my interest. The governor and I, too. But these are state secrets."

"Can this be so?" cried Goodman Brown, with a stare of amazement at his undisturbed companion. "Howbeit, I have nothing to do with the governor and council; they have their own ways, and are no rule for a simple husbandman like me. But, were I to go on with thee, how should I meet the eye of that good old man, our minister, at Salem village? Oh, his voice would make me tremble both Sabbath day and lecture day."

Thus far the elder traveler had listened with due gravity; but now burst into a fit of irrepressible mirth, shaking himself so violently that his snakelike staff actually seemed to wriggle in sympathy.

"Ha! ha! ha!" shouted he again and again; then composing himself, "Well, go on, Goodman Brown, go on; but, prithee, don't kill me with laughing."

"Well, then, to end the matter at once," said Goodman Brown, considerably nettled, "there is my wife, Faith. It would break her dear little heart; and I'd rather break my own."

"Nay, if that be the case," answered the other, "e'en go thy ways, Goodman Brown. I would not for twenty old women like the one hobbling before us that Faith should come to any harm."

As he spoke he pointed his staff at a female figure on the path, in whom Goodman Brown recognized a very pious and exemplary dame, who had taught him his catechism in youth, and was still his moral and spiritual adviser, jointly with the minister and Deacon Gookin.

"A marvel, truly, that Goody Cloyse should be so far in the wilderness at nightfall," said he. "But with your leave, friend, I shall take a cut through the woods until we have left this Christian woman behind. Being a stranger to you, she might ask whom I was consorting with and whither I was going."

"Be it so," said his fellow-traveler. "Betake you to the woods, and let me keep the path."

Accordingly the young man turned aside, but took care to watch his companion, who advanced softly along the road until he had come within a staff's length of the old dame. She, meanwhile, was making the best of her way, with singular speed for so aged a woman, and mumbling some indistinct words—a prayer, doubtless—as she went. The traveler put forth his staff and touched her withered neck with what seemed the serpent's tail.

"The devil!" screamed the pious old lady.

"Then Goody Cloyse knows her old friend?" observed the traveler, confronting her and leaning on his writhing stick.

"Ah, forsooth, and is it Your Worship indeed?" cried the good dame. "Yea, truly is it, and in the very image of my old gossip, Goodman Brown, the grandfather of the silly fellow that now is. But—would Your Worship believe it?—my broomstick hath strangely disappeared, stolen, as I suspect, by that unhanged witch, Goody Cory, and that, too, when I was all anointed with the juice of smallage, and cinquefoil, and wolf's bane."

"Mingled with fine wheat and the fat of a new-born babe," said the shape of old Goodman Brown.

"Ah, Your Worship knows the recipe," cried the old lady, cackling aloud. "So, as I was saying, being all ready for the meeting, and no horse to ride on, I made up my mind to foot it; for they tell me there is a nice young man to be taken into communion tonight. But now Your Good Worship will lend me your arm, and we shall be there in a twinkling."

"That can hardly be," answered her friend. "I may not spare you my arm, Goody Cloyse; but here is my staff, if you will."

So saying, he threw it down at her feet, where, perhaps, it assumed life, being one of the rods which its owner had formerly lent to the Egyptian magi. Of this fact, however, Goodman Brown could not take cognizance. He had cast up his eyes in astonishment, and, looking down again, beheld neither Goody Cloyse nor the serpentine staff, but his fellow-traveler alone, who waited for him as calmly as if nothing had happened.

"That old woman taught me my catechism," said the young man; and there was a world of meaning in this simple comment.

They continued to walk onward, while the elder traveler exhorted his companion to make good speed and persevere in the path, discoursing so aptly that his arguments seemed rather to spring up in the bosom of his auditor than to be suggested by himself. As they went, he plucked a branch of maple to serve for a walking stick, and began to strip it of the twigs and little boughs, which were wet with evening dew. The moment his fingers touched them they became strangely withered and dried up as with a week's sunshine. Thus the pair proceeded, at a good free pace, until suddenly, in a gloomy hollow of the road, Goodman Brown sat himself down on the stump of a tree and refused to go any farther.

"Friend," said he, stubbornly, "my mind is made up. Not another step will I budge on this errand. What if a wretched old woman do choose to go to the devil when I thought she was going to heaven: is that any reason why I should quit my dear Faith and go after her?"

"You will think better of this by and by," said his acquaintance, composedly. "Sit here and rest yourself a while; and when you feel like moving again, there is my staff to help you along."

Without more words, he threw his companion the maple stick, and was as speedily out of sight as if he had vanished into the deepening gloom. The young man sat a few moments by the roadside, applauding himself greatly, and thinking with how clear a conscience he should meet the minister in his morning walk, nor shrink from the eye of good old Deacon Gookin. And what calm sleep would be his that very night, which was to have been spent so wickedly, but so purely and sweetly now, in the arms of Faith! Amidst these pleasant and praiseworthy meditations, Goodman Brown heard the tramp of horses along the road, and deemed it advisable to conceal himself within the verge of the forest, conscious of the guilty purpose that had brought him thither, though now so happily turned from it.

On came the hoof tramps and the voices of the riders, two grave old voices, conversing soberly as they drew near. These mingled sounds appeared to pass along the road, within a few yards of the young man's hiding-place; but, owing doubtless to the depth of the gloom at that particular spot, neither the travelers nor their steeds were visible.

Though their figures brushed the small boughs by the wayside, it could not be seen that they intercepted, even for a moment, the faint gleam from the strip of bright sky athwart which they must have passed. Goodman Brown alternately crouched and stood on tiptoe, pulling aside the branches and thrusting forth his head as far as he durst without discerning so much as a shadow. It vexed him the more, because he could have sworn, were such a thing possible, that he recognized the voices of the minister and Deacon Gookin, jogging along quietly, as they were wont to do, when bound to some ordination or ecclesiastical council. While yet within hearing, one of the riders stopped to pluck a switch.

"Of the two, Reverend Sir," said the voice like the deacon's, "I had rather miss an ordination dinner than tonight's meeting. They tell me that some of our community are to be here from Falmouth and beyond, and others from Connecticut and Rhode Island, besides several of the Indian powwows, who, after their fashion, know almost as much devilry as the best of us. Moreover, there is a goodly young woman to be taken into communion."

"Mighty well, Deacon Gookin!" replied the solemn old tones of the minister. "Spur up, or we shall be late. Nothing can be done, you know, until I get on the ground."

The hoofs clattered again; and the voices, talking so strangely in the empty air, passed on through the forest, where no church had ever been gathered or solitary Christian prayed. Whither, then, could these holy men be journeying so deep into the heathen wilderness? Young Goodman Brown caught hold of a tree for support, being ready to sink down on the ground, faint and overburdened with the heavy sickness of his heart. He looked up to the sky, doubting whether there really was a heaven above him. Yet there was the blue arch, and the stars brightening in it.

"With heaven above and Faith below, I will yet stand firm against the devil!" cried Goodman Brown.

While he still gazed upward into the deep arch of the firmament and had lifted his hands to pray, a cloud, though no wind was stirring, hurried across the zenith and hid the brightening stars. The blue sky was still visible, except directly overhead, where this black mass of cloud was sweeping swiftly northward. Aloft in the air, as if from the depths of the cloud, came a confused and doubtful sound of voices. Once the listener fancied that he could distinguish the accents of towns-people of his own, men and women, both pious and ungodly, many of whom he had met at the communion table, and had seen others rioting at the tavern. The next moment, so indistinct were the sounds, he doubted whether he had heard aught but the murmur of the old forest, whispering without a wind. Then came a stronger swell of those familiar tones, heard daily in the sunshine at Salem village, but never until now from a cloud of night. There was one voice of a young woman, uttering lamentations, yet with an uncertain sorrow, and entreating for some favor, which, perhaps, it would grieve her to obtain; and all the unseen multitude, both saints and sinners, seemed to encourage her onward.

"Faith!" shouted Goodman Brown, in a voice of agony and desperation; and the echoes of the forest mocked him, crying, "Faith! Faith!" as if bewildered wretches were seeking her all through the wilderness.

The cry of grief, rage, and terror was yet piercing the night, when the unhappy husband held his breath for a response. There was a scream, drowned immediately in a louder murmur of voices, fading into far-off laughter, as the dark cloud swept away, leaving the clear and silent sky above Goodman Brown. But something fluttered lightly down through the air and caught on the branch of a tree. The young man seized it, and beheld a pink ribbon.

"My Faith is gone!" cried he, after one stupefied moment. "There is no good on earth; and sin is but a name. Come, Devil; for to thee is this world given."

And, maddened with despair, so that he laughed loud and long, did Goodman Brown grasp his staff and set forth again, at such a rate that he seemed to fly along the forest path rather than to walk or run. The road grew wilder and drearier and more faintly traced, and vanished at length, leaving him in the heart of the dark wilderness, still rushing onward with the instinct that guides mortal man to evil. The whole forest was peopled with frightful sounds—the creaking of the trees, the howling of wild beasts, and the yell of Indians; while sometimes the wind tolled like a distant church bell, and sometimes gave a broad roar around the traveler, as if all Nature were laughing him to scorn. But he was himself the chief horror of the scene, and shrank not from its other horrors.

"Ha! ha! ha!" roared Goodman Brown when the wind laughed at him.

"Let us hear which will laugh loudest. Think not to frighten me with your deviltry. Come witch, come wizard, come Indian powwow, come devil himself, and here comes Goodman Brown. You may as well fear him as he fears you."

In truth, all through the haunted forest there could be nothing more frightful than the figure of Goodman Brown. On he flew among the black pines, brandishing his staff with frenzied gestures, now giving vent to an inspiration of horrid blasphemy, and now shouting forth such laughter as set all the echoes of the forest laughing like demons around him. The fiend in his own shape is less hideous than when he rages in the breast of man. Thus sped the demoniac on his course, until, quivering among the trees, he saw a red light before him, as when the felled trunks and branches of a clearing have been set on fire, and throw up their lurid blaze against the sky, at the hour of midnight. He paused, in a lull of the tempest that had driven him onward, and heard the swell of what seemed a hymn, rolling solemnly from a distance with the weight of many voices. He knew the tune; it was a familiar one in the choir of the village meeting-house. The verse died heavily away, and was lengthened by a chorus, not of human voices, but of all the sounds of the benighted wilderness pealing in awful harmony together.

Goodman Brown cried out, and his cry was lost to his own ear by its unison with the cry of the desert.

In the interval of silence he stole forward until the light glared full upon his eyes. At one extremity of an open space, hemmed in by the dark wall of the forest, arose a rock, bearing some rude, natural resemblance either to an altar or a pulpit, and surrounded by four blazing pines, their tops aflame, their stems untouched, like candles at an evening meeting. The mass of foliage that had overgrown the summit of the rock was all on fire, blazing high into the night and fitfully illuminating the whole field. Each pendent twig and leafy festoon was in a blaze. As the red light arose and fell, a numerous congregation alternately shone forth, then disappeared in shadow, and again grew, as it were, out of the darkness, peopling the heart of the solitary woods at once.

"A grave and dark-clad company," quoth Goodman Brown.

In truth they were such. Among them, quivering to and fro between gloom and splendor, appeared faces that would be seen next day at the council board of the province, and others which, Sabbath after Sabbath, looked devoutly heavenward, and benignantly over the crowded pews, from the holiest pulpits in the land. Some affirm that the lady of the governor was there. At least there were high dames well known to her, and wives of honored husbands, and widows, a great multitude, and ancient maidens, all of excellent repute, and fair young girls, who trembled lest their mothers should espy them. Either the sudden gleams of light flashing over the obscure field bedazzled Goodman Brown, or he recognized a score of the church members of Salem village famous for their especial sanctity. Good old Deacon Gookin had arrived, and waited at the skirts of that venerable saint, his revered pastor. But, irreverently consorting with these grave, reputable, and pious people, these elders of the church, these chaste dames and dewy virgins, there were men of dissolute lives and women of spotted fame, wretches given over to all mean and filthy vice, and suspected even of horrid crimes. It was strange to see that the good shrank not from the wicked, nor were the sinners abashed by the saints. Scattered also among their pale-faced enemies were the Indian priests, or powwows, who had often scared their native forest with more hideous incantations than any known to English witchcraft.

"But where is Faith?" thought Goodman Brown; and, as hope came into his heart, he trembled.

Another verse of the hymn arose, a slow and mournful strain, such as the pious love, but joined to words which expressed all that our nature can conceive of sin, and darkly hinted at far more. Unfathomable to mere mortals is the lore of fiends. Verse after verse was sung; and still the chorus of the desert swelled between like the deepest tone of a mighty organ; and with the final peal of that dreadful anthem there came a sound, as if the roaring wind, the rushing streams, the howling beasts, and every other voice of the unconcerted wilderness were mingling and according with the voice of guilty man in homage to the prince of all. The four blazing pines threw up a loftier flame, and obscurely discovered shapes and visages of horror on the smoke wreaths above the impious assembly. At the same moment the fire on the rock shot redly forth and formed a glowing arch above its base, where now appeared a figure. With reverence be it spoken, the figure bore no slight similitude, both in garb and manner, to some grave divine of the New England churches.

"Bring forth the converts!" cried a voice that echoed through the field and rolled into the forest.

At the word, Goodman Brown stepped forth from the shadow of the trees and approached the congregation, with whom he felt a loathful brotherhood by the sympathy of all that was wicked in his heart. He could have well-nigh sworn that the shape of his own dead father beckoned him to advance, looking downward from a smoke wreath, while a woman, with dim features of despair, threw out her hand to warn him back. Was it his mother? But he had no power to retreat one step, nor to resist, even in thought, when the minister and good old Deacon Gookin seized his arms and led him to the blazing rock. Thither came also the slender form of a veiled female, led between Goody Cloyse, that pious teacher of the catechism, and Martha Carrier, who had received the devil's promise to be queen of hell. A rampant hag was she. And there stood the proselytes beneath the canopy of fire.

"Welcome, my children," said the dark figure, "to the communion of your race. Ye have found thus young your nature and your destiny. My children, look behind you!"

They turned; and flashing forth, as it were, in a sheet of flame, the fiend worshippers were seen; the smile of welcome gleamed darkly on every visage.

"There," resumed the sable form, "are all whom ye have reverenced from youth. Ye deemed them holier than yourselves, and shrank from your own sin, contrasting it with their lives of righteousness and prayerful aspirations heavenward. Yet here are they all in my worshipping assembly. This night it shall be granted you to know their secret deeds: how hoary-bearded elders of the church have whispered wanton words to the young maids of their households; how many a woman, eager for widows' weeds, has given her husband a drink at bedtime and let him sleep his last sleep in her bosom; how beardless youths have made haste to inherit their fathers' wealth; and how fair damsels—blush not, sweet ones—have dug little graves in the garden, and bidden me, the sole guest to an infant's funeral. By the sympathy of your human hearts for sin ye shall scent out all the places—whether in church, bedchamber, street, field, or forest—where crime has been committed, and shall exult to behold the whole earth one stain of guilt, one mighty blood spot. Far more than this. It shall be yours to penetrate, in every bosom, the deep mystery of sin, the fountain of all wicked arts, and which inexhaustibly supplies more evil impulses than human power—than my power at its utmost—can make manifest in deeds. And now, my children, look upon each other."

They did so; and, by the blaze of the hell-kindled torches, the wretched man beheld his Faith, and the wife her husband, trembling before that unhallowed altar.

"Lo, there ye stand, my children," said the figure, in a deep and solemn tone, almost sad with its despairing awfulness, as if his once angelic nature could yet mourn for our miserable race. "Depending upon one another's hearts, ye had still hoped that virtue were not all a dream. Now are ye undeceived. Evil is the nature of mankind. Evil must be your only happiness. Welcome again, my children, to the communion of your race."

"Welcome," repeated the fiend worshippers, in one cry of despair and triumph.

And there they stood, the only pair, as it seemed, who were yet hesitating on the verge of wickedness in this dark world. A basin was hollowed, naturally, in the rock. Did it contain water, reddened by the lurid light? or was it blood? or, perchance, a liquid flame? Herein did the shape of evil dip his hand and prepare to lay the mark of baptism upon their foreheads, that they might be partakers of the mystery of sin, more conscious of the secret guilt of others, both in deed and thought, than they could now be of their own. The husband cast one look at his pale wife, and Faith at him. What polluted wretches would the next glance show them to each other, shuddering alike at what they disclosed and what they saw!

"Faith! Faith!" cried the husband; "look up to heaven, and resist the wicked one."

Whether Faith obeyed he knew not. Hardly had he spoken when he found himself amid calm night and solitude, listening to a roar of the wind which died heavily away through the forest. He staggered against the rock, and felt it chill and damp; while a hanging twig, that had been all on fire, besprinkled his cheek with the coldest dew.

The next morning young Goodman Brown came slowly into the street of Salem village, staring around him like a bewildered man. The good old minister was taking a walk along the graveyard to get an appetite for breakfast and meditate his sermon, and bestowed a blessing, as he passed, on Goodman Brown. He shrank from the venerable saint as if to avoid an anathema. Old Deacon Gookin was at domestic worship, and the holy words of his prayer were heard through the open window. "What God doth the wizard pray to?" quoth Goodman Brown. Goody Cloyse, that excellent old Christian, stood in the early sunshine at her own lattice, catechizing a little girl who had brought her a pint of morning's milk. Goodman Brown snatched away the child as from the grasp of the fiend himself. Turning the corner by the meeting-house, he spied the head of Faith, with the pink ribbons, gazing anxiously forth, and bursting into such joy at sight of him that she skipped along the street and almost kissed her husband before the whole village. But Goodman Brown looked sternly and sadly into her face, and passed on without a greeting.

Had Goodman Brown fallen asleep in the forest and only dreamed a wild dream of a witch-meeting?

Be it so if you will; but, alas! It was a dream of evil omen for young Goodman Brown. A stern, a sad, a darkly meditative, a distrustful, if not a desperate man did he become from the night of that fearful dream. On the Sabbath day, when the congregation were singing a holy Psalm, he could not listen because an anthem of sin rushed loudly upon his ear and drowned all the blessed strain. When the minister spoke from the pulpit with power and fervid eloquence, and, with his hand on the open Bible, of the sacred truths of our religion, and of saint-like lives and triumphant deaths, and of future bliss or misery unutterable, then did Goodman Brown turn pale, dreading lest the roof should thunder down upon the gray blasphemer and his hearers. Often, waking suddenly at midnight, he shrank from the bosom of Faith; and at morning or eventide, when the family knelt down at prayer, he scowled and muttered to himself, and gazed sternly at his wife, and turned away. And when he had lived long, and was borne to his grave a hoary corpse, followed by Faith, an aged woman, and children and grandchildren, a goodly procession, besides neighbors not a few, they carved no hopeful verse upon his tombstone, for his dying hour was gloom.

Nikolai Gogol
(1809-1852)

Introduction
"Viy"

Born the same year as Edgar Allan Poe, Nikolai Gogol was one of the most influential figures in Russian horror literature for the first half of the 1800s. "Viy" (Gnome King) was first published in volume 2 of Gogol's collection of short stories, *Mirgorod*, in 1835. To date, there has never been an account found of a gnome king named "Viy" in Ukrainian folklore or legend. As a result, the term Viy is considered a fiction of Gogol's fantastic imagination.

"Viy" is a classic witch tale set in a remote Ukrainian village. It was first translated into English by Claud Field during 1916 in an anthology of Gogol's short works, *The Mantle and Other Stories*. This marked nearly eighty years before "Viy" had markedly influenced English-speaking authors.

The story broke new ground in exploring themes of faith, power, the human psyche, and life after death. Nearly two hundred years after its first publication, there is no question that "Viy" has sustained an enduring legacy in the world of horror and fantasy literature.

This is what Field had to say about it, and he is spot on. "The receipt for a good, fantastic tale is well known: begin with well-defined portraits of eccentric characters, but such as to be within the bounds of possibility, described with minute realism. From the grotesque to the marvellous the transition is imperceptible, and the reader will find himself in the world of fantasy before he perceives that he has left the real world far behind him. I purposely avoid any attempt to analyse 'The King of the Gnomes'; the proper time and place to read it is in the country, by the fireside on a stormy autumn night. After the denouement, it will require a certain amount of resolution to traverse long corridors to reach one's room, while the wind and the rain shake the casements. Now that the fantastic style of the Germans is a little threadbare, that of the Cossacks will have novel charms, and in the first place the merit of resembling nothing else — no slight praise, I think."

"Viy" is likely the first great Russian witch short story and I hope you read it "by the fireside on a stormy autumn night."

Viy
1835

(The "Viy" is a monstrous creation of popular fancy. It is the name which the inhabitants of Little Russia give to the king of the gnomes, whose eyelashes reach to the ground. The following story is a specimen of such folk-lore. I have made no alterations, but reproduce it in the same simple form in which I heard it. — Author's Note.)

I

AS SOON AS the clear seminary bell began sounding in Kieff[10] in the morning, the pupils would come flocking from all parts of the town. The students of grammar, rhetoric,

---

[10] More commonly, "Kiev," is the largest city in the country of Ukraine.

philosophy, and theology hastened with their books under their arms over the streets.

The "grammarians" were still mere boys. On the way they pushed against each other and quarrelled with shrill voices. Nearly all of them wore torn or dirty clothes, and their pockets were always crammed with all kinds of things — push-bones, pipes made out of pens, remains of confectionery, and sometimes even young sparrows. The latter would sometimes begin to chirp in the midst of deep silence in the school, and bring down on their possessors severe canings and thrashings.

The "rhetoricians" walked in a more orderly way. Their clothes were generally untorn, but on the other hand their faces were often strangely decorated; one had a black eye, and the lips of another resembled a single blister, etc. These spoke to each other in tenor voices.

The "philosophers" talked in a tone an octave lower; in their pockets they only had fragments of tobacco, never whole cakes of it; for what they could get hold of, they used at once. They smelt so strongly of tobacco and brandy, that a workman passing by them would often remain standing and sniffing with his nose in the air, like a hound.

About this time of day the market-place was generally full of bustle, and the market women, selling rolls, cakes, and honey-tarts, plucked the sleeves of those who wore coats of fine cloth or cotton.

"Young sir! Young sir! Here! Here!" they cried from all sides. "Rolls and cakes and tasty tarts, very delicious! I have baked them myself!"

Another drew something long and crooked out of her basket and cried, "Here is a sausage, young sir! Buy a sausage!"

"Don't buy anything from her!" cried a rival. "See how greasy she is, and what a dirty nose and hands she has!"

But the market women carefully avoided appealing to the philosophers and theologians, for these only took handfuls of eatables merely to taste them.

Arrived at the seminary, the whole crowd of students dispersed into the low, large class-rooms with small windows, broad doors, and blackened benches. Suddenly they were filled
with a many-toned murmur. The teachers heard the pupils' lessons repeated, some in shrill and others in deep voices which sounded like a distant booming. While the lessons were being said, the teachers kept a sharp eye open to see

whether pieces of cake or other dainties were protruding from their pupils' pockets; if so, they were promptly confiscated.

When this learned crowd arrived somewhat earlier than usual, or when it was known that the teachers would come somewhat late, a battle would ensue, as though planned by general agreement. In this battle all had to take part, even the monitors who were appointed to look after the order and morality of the whole school.

Two theologians generally arranged the conditions of the battle: whether each class should split into two sides, or whether all the pupils should divide themselves into two halves.

In each case the grammarians began the battle, and after the rhetoricians had joined in, the former retired and stood on the benches, in order to watch the fortunes of the fray. Then came
the philosophers with long black moustaches, and finally the thick-necked theologians. The battle generally ended in a victory for the latter, and the philosophers retired to the different class-rooms rubbing their aching limbs, and throwing themselves on the benches to take breath.

When the teacher, who in his own time had taken part in such contests, entered the class-room he saw by the heated faces of his pupils that the battle had been very severe, and while he caned the hands of the rhetoricians, in another room another teacher did the same for the philosophers.

On Sundays and Festival Days the seminarists took puppet- theatres to the citizens' houses. Sometimes they acted a comedy, and in that case it was always a theologian who took the part of the hero or heroine — Potiphar or Herodias, etc. As a reward for their exertions, they received a piece of linen, a sack of maize, half a roast goose, or something similar. All the students, lay and clerical, were very poorly provided with means for procuring themselves necessary subsistence, but at the same time very fond of eating; so that, however much food was given to them, they were never satisfied, and the gifts bestowed by rich landowners were never adequate for their needs.

Therefore the Commissariat Committee, consisting of philosophers and theologians, sometimes dispatched the grammarians and rhetoricians under the leadership of a philosopher — themselves sometimes joining in the expedition — with sacks on their shoulders, into the town, in order to levy a contribution on the neshpots of the citizens, and then there was a feast in the seminary.

The most important event in the seminary year was the arrival of the holidays; these began in July, and then generally all the students went home. At that time all the roads were thronged with grammarians, rhetoricians, philosophers, and theologians. He who had no home of his own would take up his quarters with some fellow-student's family; the philosophers and theologians looked out for tutors' posts, taught the children of rich farmers, and received for doing so a pair of new boots and sometimes also a new coat.

A whole troop of them would go off in close ranks like a regiment; they cooked their porridge in common, and encamped under the open sky. Each had a bag with him containing a shirt and a pair of socks. The theologians were especially economical; in order not to wear out their boots too quickly, they took them off and carried them on a stick over their shoulders, especially when the road was very muddy. Then they tucked up their breeches over their knees and waded bravely through the pools and puddles. Whenever they spied a village near the highway, they at once left it, approached the house which seemed the most considerable, and began with loud voices to sing a psalm. The master of the house, an old Cossack engaged in agriculture, would listen for a long time with his head propped in his hands, then with tears on his cheeks say to his wife, "What the students are singing sounds very devout; bring out some lard and anything else of the kind we have in the house."

After thus replenishing their stores, the students would continue their way. The farther they went, the smaller grew their numbers, as they dispersed to their various houses, and left those whose homes were still farther on.

On one occasion, during such a march, three students left the main-road in order to get provisions in some village, since their stock had long been exhausted. This party consisted of the theologian Khalava, the philosopher Thomas Brutus, and the rhetorician Tiberius Gorobetz.

The first was a tall youth with broad shoulders and of a peculiar character; everything which came within reach of his fingers he felt obliged to appropriate. Moreover, he was of a very melancholy disposition, and when he had got intoxicated he hid himself in the most tangled thickets so that the seminary officials had the greatest trouble in finding him.

The philosopher Thomas Brutus was a more cheerful character. He liked to lie for a long time on the same spot and smoke his pipe; and when he was merry with wine, he hired a fiddler and danced the "tropak."[11] Often he got a whole quantity of "beans," i.e. thrashings; but these he endured with complete philosophic calm, saying that a man cannot escape his destiny.

The rhetorician Tiberius Gorobetz had not yet the right to wear a moustache, to drink brandy, or to smoke tobacco. He only wore a small crop of hair, as though his character was at present too little developed. To judge by the great bumps on his forehead, with which he often appeared in the class-room, it might be expected that some day he would be a valiant fighter. Khalava and Thomas often pulled his hair as a mark of their special favour, and sent him on their errands.

Evening had already come when they left the high-road; the sun had just gone down, and the air was still heavy with the heat of the day. The theologian and the philosopher strolled along, smoking in silence, while the rhetorician struck off the heads of the thistles by the wayside with his stick. The way wound on through thick woods of oak and walnut; green hills alternated here and there with meadows. Twice already they had seen cornfields, from which they concluded that they were near some village; but an hour had already passed, and no human habitation appeared. The sky was already quite dark, and only a red gleam lingered on the western horizon.

"The deuce!" said the philosopher Thomas Brutus. "I was almost certain we would soon reach a village."

The theologian still remained silent, looked round him, then put his pipe again between his teeth, and all three continued their way.

"Good heavens!" exclaimed the philosopher, and stood still. "Now the road itself is disappearing."

"Perhaps we shall find a farm farther on," answered the theologian, without taking his pipe out of his mouth.

Meanwhile the night had descended; clouds increased the darkness, and according to all appearance there was no

---

[11] A traditional, high step folk dance that started in Ukraine and was adopted by the Russians.

chance of moon or stars appearing. The seminarists found that they had lost the way altogether.

After the philosopher had vainly sought for a footpath, he exclaimed, "Where have we got to?"

The theologian thought for a while, and said, "Yes, it is really dark."

The rhetorician went on one side, lay on the ground, and groped for a path; but his hands encountered only fox-holes. All around lay a huge steppe over which no one seemed to have passed. The wanderers made several efforts to get forward, but the landscape grew wilder and more inhospitable.

The philosopher tried to shout, but his voice was lost in vacancy, no one answered; only, some moments later, they heard a faint groaning sound, like the whimpering of a wolf.

"Curse it all! What shall we do?" said the philosopher.

"Why, just stop here, and spend the night in the open air," answered the theologian. So saying, he felt in his pocket, brought out his timber and steel, and lit his pipe.

But the philosopher could not agree with this proposal; he was not accustomed to sleep till he had first eaten five pounds of bread and five of dripping, and so he now felt an intolerable emptiness in his stomach. Besides, in spite of his cheerful temperament, he was a little afraid of the wolves.

"No, Khalava," he said, "that won't do. To lie down like a dog and without any supper! Let us try once more; perhaps we shall find a house, and the consolation of having a glass of brandy to drink before going to sleep."

At the word "brandy," the theologian spat on one side and said, "Yes, of course, we cannot remain all night in the open air."

The students went on and on, and to their great joy they heard the barking of dogs in the distance. After listening a while to see from which direction the barking came, they went on their way with new courage, and soon espied a light.

"A village, by heavens, a village!" exclaimed the philosopher.

His supposition proved correct; they soon saw two or three houses built round a court-yard. Lights glimmered in the windows, and before the fence stood a number of trees. The students looked through the crevices of the gates and saw a court-yard in which stood a large number of roving tradesmen's carts. In the sky there were now fewer clouds, and here and there a star was visible.

"See, brother!" one of them said, "we must now cry 'halt!' Cost what it may, we must find entrance and a night's lodging."

The three students knocked together at the gate, and cried "Open!"

The door of one of the houses creaked on its hinges, and an old woman wrapped in a sheepskin appeared. "Who is there?" she exclaimed, coughing loudly.

"Let us spend the night here, mother; we have lost our way, our stomachs are empty, and we do not want to spend the night out of doors."

"But what sort of people are you?"

"Quite harmless people; the theologian Khalava, the philosopher Brutus, and the rhetorician Gorobetz."

"It is impossible," answered the old woman. "The whole house is full of people, and every corner occupied. Where can I put you up? You are big and heavy enough to break the house

down. I know these philosophers and theologians; when one takes them in, they eat one out of house and home. Go farther on! There is no room here for you!"

"Have pity on us, mother! How can you be so heartless? Don't let Christians perish. Put us up where you like, and if we eat up your pro-visions, or do any other damage, may our hands wither up, and all the punishment of heaven light on us!"

The old woman seemed a little touched. "Well," she said after a few moments' consideration, "I will let you in; but I must put you in different rooms, for I should have no quiet if you were all together at night."

"Do just as you like; we won't say any more about it," answered the students.

The gates moved heavily on their hinges, and they entered the court-yard.

"Well now, mother," said the philosopher, following the old woman, "if you had a little scrap of something! By heavens! my stomach is as empty as a drum. I have not had a bit of bread in my mouth since early this morning!"

"Didn't I say so?" replied the old woman.

"There you go begging at once. But I have no food in the house, nor any fire."

"But we will pay for everything," continued the philosopher.

"We will pay early to-morrow in cash."

"Go on and be content with what you get. You are fine fellows whom the devil has brought here!"

Her reply greatly depressed the philosopher Thomas; but suddenly his nose caught the odour of dried fish; he looked at the breeches of the theologian, who walked by his side, and saw a huge fish's tail sticking out of his pocket. The latter had already seized the opportunity to steal a whole fish from one of the carts standing in the court-yard. He had not done this from hunger so much as from the force of habit. He had quite forgotten the fish, and was looking about to see whether he could not find something else to appropriate. Then the philosopher put his hand in the theologian's pocket as though it were his own, and laid hold of his prize.

The old woman found a special resting-place for each student; the rhetorician she put in a shed, the theologian in an empty store-room, and the philosopher in a sheep's stall. As soon as the philosopher was alone, he devoured the fish in a twinkling, examined the fence which enclosed the stall, kicked away a pig from a neighbouring stall, which had inquiringly inserted its nose through a crevice, and lay down on his right side to sleep like a corpse.

Then the low door opened, and the old woman came crouching into the stall.

"Well, mother, what do you want here?" asked the philosopher.

She made no answer, but came with outstretched arms towards him.

The philosopher shrank back; but she still approached, as though she wished to lay hold of him. A terrible fright seized him, for he saw the old hag's eyes sparkle in an extraordinary way. "Away with you, old witch, away with you!" he shouted. But she still stretched her hands after him.

He jumped up in order to rush out, but she placed herself before the door, fixed her glowing eyes upon him, and again approached him. The philosopher tried to push her away with his

hands, but to his astonishment he found that he could neither lift his hands nor move his legs, nor utter an audible word. He only heard his heart beating, and saw the old woman approach him, place his hands crosswise on his breast, and bend his head down. Then with the agility of a cat she sprang on his shoulders, struck him in the side with a broom, and he began to run like a race-horse, carrying her on his shoulders.

All this happened with such swiftness, that the philosopher could scarcely collect his thoughts. He laid hold of his knees with both hands in order to stop his legs from running; but to his great astonishment they kept moving forward against his will, making rapid springs like a Caucasian horse.

Not till the house had been left behind them and a wide plain stretched before them, bordered on one side by a black gloomy wood, did he say to himself, "Ah! it is a witch!"

The half -moon shone pale and high in the sky. Its mild light, still more subdued by intervening clouds, fell like a transparent veil on the earth. Woods, meadows, hills, and valleys — all seemed to be sleeping with open eyes; nowhere was a breath of air stirring. The atmosphere was moist and warm; the shadows of the trees and bushes fell sharply defined on the sloping plain. Such was the night through which the philosopher Thomas Brutus sped with his strange rider.

A strange, oppressive, and yet sweet sensation took possession of his heart. He looked down and saw how the grass beneath his feet seemed to be quite deep and far away; over it there flowed a flood of crystal-clear water, and the grassy plain looked like the bottom of a transparent sea. He saw his own image, and that of the old woman whom he carried on his back,
clearly reflected in it. Then he beheld how, instead of the moon, a strange sun shone there; he heard the deep tones of bells, and saw them swinging. He saw a water-nixie[12] rise from a bed of tall reeds; she turned to him, and her face was clearly visible, and she sang a song which penetrated his soul; then she approached him
and nearly reached the surface of the water, on which she burst into laughter and again disappeared.

Did he see it or did he not see it? Was he dreaming or was he awake? But what was that below — wind or music? It sounded and drew nearer, and penetrated his soul like a song that rose and fell. "What is it?" he thought as he gazed into the depths, and still sped rapidly along.

The perspiration flowed from him in streams; he experienced simultaneously a strange feeling of oppression and delight in all his being. Often he felt as though he had

---

[12] A water spirit, typically with the head and torso of a woman.

no longer a heart, and pressed his hand on his breast with alarm.

Weary to death, he began to repeat all the prayers which he knew, and all the formulas of exorcism against evil spirits. Suddenly he experienced a certain relief. He felt that his pace was slackening; the witch weighed less heavily on his shoulders, and the thick herbage of the plain was again beneath his feet, with nothing especial to remark about it, "Splendid!" thought the philosopher Thomas, and began to repeat his exorcisms in a
still louder voice.

Then suddenly he wrenched himself away from under the witch, and sprang on her back in his turn. She began to run, with short, trembling steps indeed, but so rapidly that he could hardly
breathe. So swiftly did she run that she hardly seemed to touch the ground. They were still on the plain, but owing to the rapidity of their flight everything seemed indistinct and confused before his eyes. He seized a stick that was lying on the ground, and began to belabour the hag with all his might. She uttered a wild cry, which at first sounded raging and threatening; then it became gradually weaker and more gentle, till at last it sounded quite low like the pleasant tones of a silver bell, so that it penetrated his innermost soul. Involuntarily the thought passed through his mind, "Is she really an old woman?"

"Ah! I can go no farther," she said in a faint voice, and sank to the earth.

He knelt beside her, and looked in her eyes. The dawn was red in the sky, and in the distance glimmered the gilt domes of the churches of Kieff. Before him lay a beautiful maiden with thick, dishevelled hair and long eyelashes. Unconsciously she had stretched out her white, bare arms, and her tear-filled eyes gazed at the sky.

Thomas trembled like an aspen-leaf. Sympathy, and a strange feeling of excitement, and a hitherto unknown fear overpowered him. He began to run with all his might. His heart beat violently, and he could not explain to himself what a strange, new feeling had seized him. He did not wish to return to the village, but hastened towards Kieff, thinking all the way as he went, of his weird, unaccountable adventure.

There were hardly any students left in the town; they were all scattered about the country, and had either taken tutors' posts or simply lived without occupation; for at the farms in Little Russia one can live comfortably and at ease without paying a farthing. The great half-decayed building in which the seminary was established was completely empty; and however much the philosopher searched in all its corners for a piece of lard and bread, he could not find even one of the hard biscuits which the seminarists were in the habit of hiding.

But the philosopher found a means of extricating himself from his difficulties by making friends with a certain young widow in the market-place who sold ribbons, etc. The same evening he found himself being stuffed with cakes and fowl; in fact it is impossible to say how many things were placed before him on a little table in an arbour shaded by cherry-trees.

Later, on the same evening the philosopher was to be seen in an ale-house. He lay on a bench, smoked his pipe in his usual way, and threw the Jewish publican a gold piece. He had a jug of ale standing before him, looked on all who went in and out in a cold-blooded, self-satisfied way, and thought no more of his strange adventure.

About this time a report spread about that the daughter of a rich colonel, whose estate lay about fifty versts[13] distant from Kieff, had returned home one day from a walk in a quite broken-down condition. She had scarcely enough strength to reach her father's house; now she lay dying, and had expressed a wish that for three days after her death the prayers for the dead should be recited by a Kieff seminarist named Thomas Brutus.

This fact was communicated to the philosopher by the rector of the seminary himself, who sent for him to his room and told him that he must start at once, as a rich colonel had sent his servants and a kibitka for him. The philosopher trembled, and was seized by an uncomfortable feeling which he could not define. He had a gloomy foreboding that some evil was about to befall him. Without knowing why, he declared that he did not wish to go.

"Listen, Thomas," said the rector, who under certain circumstances spoke very politely to his pupils; "I have no idea of asking you whether you wish to go or not. I only tell you that if you think of disobeying, I will have you so soundly flogged on the back with young birch-rods, that you need not think of having a bath for a long time."

---

[13] A verst is 1.1 kilometers or 0.66 miles, which means 50 versts would equal 55 kilometers or 33 miles.

The philosopher scratched the back of his head, and went out silently, intending to make himself scarce at the first opportunity. Lost in thought, he descended the steep flight of steps which led to the court-yard, thickly planted with poplars; there he remained standing for a moment, and heard quite distinctly the rector giving orders in a loud voice to his steward,

and to another person, probably one of the messengers sent by the colonel.

"Thank your master for the peeled barley and the eggs," said the rector; "and tell him that as soon as the books which he mentions in his note are ready, I will send them. I have already given them to a clerk to be copied. And don't forget to remind your master that he has some excellent fish, especially prime sturgeon, in his ponds; he might send me some when he has the

opportunity, as here in the market the fish are bad and dear. And you, Jantukh, give the colonel's man a glass of brandy. And mind you tie up the philosopher, or he will show you a clean pair of heels."

"Listen to the scoundrel!" thought the philosopher. "He has smelt a rat, the long-legged stork!"

He descended into the court-yard and beheld there a kibitka,[14] which he at first took for a barn on wheels. It was, in fact, as roomy as a kiln, so that bricks might have been made inside it. It was one of those remarkable Cracow vehicles in which Jews travelled from town to town in scores, wherever they thought they would find a market. Six stout, strong, though somewhat elderly Cossacks were standing by it. Their gold-braided coats of fine cloth showed that their master was rich and of some importance; and certain little scars testified to their valour on the battle-field.

"What can I do?" thought the philosopher. "There is no escaping one's destiny!" So he stepped up to the Cossacks and said "Good day, comrades."

"Welcome, Mr Philosopher!" some of them answered.

"Well, I am to travel with you! It is a magnificent vehicle," he continued as he got into it. "If there were only musicians present, one might dance in it."

"Yes, it is a roomy carriage," said one of the Cossacks, taking his seat by the coachman. The latter had tied a cloth

---

[14] A large Russian or Ukrainian carriage drawn by horses.

round his head, as he had already found an opportunity of pawning his cap in the ale-house. The other five, with the philosopher, got into the capacious kibitka, and sat upon sacks which were filled with all sorts of articles purchased in the city.

"I should like to know," said the philosopher, "if this equipage were laden with salt or iron, how many horses would be required to draw it?"

"Yes," said the Cossack who sat by the coachman, after thinking a short time, "it would require a good many horses."

After giving this satisfactory answer, the Cossack considered himself entitled to remain silent for the whole of the rest of the journey.

The philosopher would gladly have found out who the colonel was, and what sort of a character he had. He was also curious to know about his daughter, who had returned home in such a strange way and now lay dying, and whose destiny seemed to be mingled with his own; and wanted to know the sort of life that was lived in the colonel's house. But the Cossacks were probably philosophers like himself, for in answer to his inquiries they only blew clouds of tobacco and settled themselves more comfortably on their sacks.

Meanwhile, one of them addressed to the coachman on the box a brief command, "Keep your eyes open, Overko, you old sleepy-head, and when you come to the ale-house on the road to Tchukrailoff, don't forget to pull up and wake me and the other fellows if we are asleep." Then he began to snore pretty loud. But in any case his admonition was quite superfluous; for scarcely had the enormous equipage begun to approach the aforesaid ale-house, than they all cried with one mouth, "Halt! Halt!" Besides this, Overko's horse was accustomed to stop outside every inn of its own accord.

In spite of the intense July heat, they all got out and entered a low, dirty room where a Jewish innkeeper received them in a friendly way as old acquaintances. He brought in the skirt of his long coat some sausages, and laid them on the table, where, though forbidden by the Talmud,[15] they looked very seductive. All sat down at table, and it was not long before each of the guests had an

---

[15] The main text on Rabbinic Judaism that clarifies points in the Hebrew Bible.

earthenware jug standing in front of him. The philosopher Thomas had to take part in the feast, and as the Little Eussians when they are intoxicated always begin to kiss each other or to weep, the whole room soon began to echo with demonstrations of affection.

"Come here, come here, Spirid, let me embrace thee!"

"Come here, Dorosch, let me press you to my heart!"

One Cossack, with a grey moustache, the eldest of them all, leant his head on his hand and began to weep bitterly because he was an orphan and alone in God's wide world. Another tall, loquacious man did his best to comfort him, saying, "Don't weep, for God's sake, don't weep! For over there — God knows best."

The Cossack who had been addressed as Dorosch was full of curiosity, and addressed many questions to the philosopher Thomas. "I should like to know," he said, "what you learn in your seminary; do you learn the same things as the deacon reads to us in church, or something else?"

"Don't ask," said the consoler; "let them learn what they like. God knows what is to happen; God knows everything."

"No, I will know," answered Dorosch, "I will know what is written in their books; perhaps it is something quite different from that in the deacon's book."

"Good heavens!" said the other, "why all this talk? It is God's will, and one cannot change God's arrangements."

"But I will know everything that is written; I will enter the seminary too, by heaven I will! Do you think perhaps I could not learn? I will learn everything, everything."

"Oh, heavens!" exclaimed the consoler, and let his head sink on the table, for he could no longer hold it upright.

The other Cossacks talked about the nobility, and why there was a moon in the sky.

When the philosopher Thomas saw the state they were in, he determined to profit by it, and to make his escape. In the first place he turned to the grey-headed Cossack, who was lamenting the loss of his parents. "But, little uncle," he said to him, "Why do you weep so? I too am an orphan! Let me go, children; why do you want me?"

"Let him go!" said some of them, "he is an orphan, let him go where he likes."

They were about to take him outside themselves, when the one who had displayed a special thirst for knowledge, stopped them, saying, "No, I want to talk with him about the seminary; I am going to the seminary myself."

Moreover, it was not yet certain whether the philosopher could have executed his project of flight, for when he tried to rise from his chair, he felt as though his feet were made of wood, and he began to see such a number of doors leading out of the room that it would have been difficult for him to have found the right one.

It was not till evening that the company remembered that they must continue their journey. They crowded into the kibitka, whipped up the horses, and struck up a song, the words and sense of which were hard to understand. During a great part of the night, they wandered about, having lost the road which they ought to have been able to find blindfolded. At last they drove down a steep descent into a valley, and the philosopher noticed, by the sides of the road, hedges, behind which he caught glimpses of small trees and house-roofs. All these belonged to the colonel's estate.

It was already long past midnight. The sky was dark, though little stars glimmered here and there; no light was to be seen in any of the houses. They drove into a large court-yard, while the dogs barked. On all sides were barns and cottages with thatched roofs. Just opposite the gateway was a house, which was larger than the others, and seemed to be the colonel's dwelling. The kibitka stopped before a small barn, and the travellers hastened into it and laid themselves down to sleep. The philosopher how- ever attempted to look at the exterior of the house, but, rub his eyes as he might, he could distinguish nothing; the house seemed to turn into a bear, and the chimney into the rector of the seminary. Then he gave it up and lay down to sleep.

When he woke up the next morning, the whole house was in commotion; the young lady had died during the night. The servants ran hither and thither in a distracted state; the old women wept and lamented; and a number of curious people gazed through the enclosure into the court-yard, as though there were something special to be seen. The philosopher began now to inspect the locality and the buildings, which he had not been able to do during the night.

The colonel's house was one of those low, small buildings, such as used formerly to be constructed in Eussia. It was thatched with straw; a small, high-peaked gable, with a window shaped like an eye, was painted all over with blue and yellow flowers and red crescent-moons; it rested on little oaken pillars, which were round above the middle, hexagonal below, and whose capitals were adorned with quaint carvings. Under this gable was a small staircase with seats at the foot of it on either side.

The walls of the house were supported by similar pillars. Before the house stood a large pear-tree of pyramidal shape, whose leaves incessantly trembled. A double row of buildings formed a broad street leading up to the colonel's house. Behind the barns near the entrance-gate stood two three-cornered wine-houses, also thatched with straw; each of the stone walls had a door in it, and was covered with all kinds of paintings. On one was represented a Cossack sitting on a barrel and swinging a large pitcher over his head; it bore the inscription "I will drink all that!"

Elsewhere were painted large and small bottles, a beautiful girl, a running horse, a pipe, and a drum bearing the words "Wine is the Cossack's joy."

In the loft of one of the barns one saw through a huge round window a drum and some trumpets. At the gate there stood two cannons. All this showed that the colonel loved a cheerful life, and the whole place often rang with sounds of merriment. Before the gate were two windmills, and behind the house gardens sloped away; through the tree-tops the dark chimneys of the peasants' houses were visible. The whole village lay on a broad, even plateau, in the middle of a mountain-slope which culminated in a steep summit on the north side. When seen from below, it looked still steeper. Here and there on the top the irregular stems of the thick steppe-brooms showed in dark relief against the blue sky. The bare clay soil made a melancholy impression, worn as it was into deep furrows by rain-water. On the same slope there stood two cottages, and over one of them a huge apple-tree spread its branches; the roots were supported by small props, whose interstices were filled with mould. The apples, which were blown off by the wind, rolled down to the court-yard below. A road wound round the mountain to the village.

When the philosopher looked at this steep slope, and remembered his journey of the night before, he came to the conclusion that either the colonel's horses were very sagacious, or that the Cossacks must have very strong heads, as they ventured, even when the worse for drink, on such a road with the huge kibitka.

When the philosopher turned and looked in the opposite direction, he saw quite another picture. The village reached down to the plain; meadows stretched away to an immense distance, their bright green growing gradually dark; far away, about twenty versts off, many other villages were visible. To the right of these meadows were chains of hills, and in the remote distance one saw the Dnieper shimmer and sparkle like a mirror of steel.

"What a splendid country!" said the philosopher to himself. "It must be fine to live here! One could catch fish in the Dnieper, and in the ponds, and shoot and snare partridges and bustards; there must be quantities here. Much fruit might be dried here and sold in the town, or, better still, brandy might be distilled from it, for fruit-brandy is the best of all. But what prevents me thinking of my escape after all?"

Behind the hedge he saw a little path which was almost entirely concealed by the high grass of the steppe. The philosopher approached it mechanically, meaning at first to walk a little along it unobserved, and then quite quietly to gain the open country behind the peasants' houses. Suddenly he felt the pressure of a fairly heavy hand on his shoulder.

Behind him stood the same old Cossack who yesterday had so bitterly lamented the death of his father and mother, and his own loneliness. "You are giving yourself useless trouble, Mr Philosopher, if you think you can escape from us," he said. "One cannot run away here; and besides, the roads are too bad for walkers. Come to the colonel; he has been waiting for you for some time in his room."

"Yes, of course! What are you talking about? I will come with the greatest pleasure," said the philosopher, and followed the Cossack.

The colonel was an elderly man; his moustache was grey, and his face wore the signs of deep sadness. He sat in his room by a table, with his head propped on both hands. He seemed about five-and-fifty, but his attitude of utter despair, and the pallor on his face, showed that his heart had been suddenly broken, and that all his former cheerfulness had for ever disappeared.

When Thomas entered with the Cossack, he answered their deep bows with a slight inclination of the head.

"Who are you, whence do you come, and what is your profession, my good man?" asked the colonel in an even voice, neither friendly nor austere.

"I am a student of philosophy; my name is Thomas Brutus."

"And who was your father?"

"I don't know, sir."

"And your mother?"

"I don't know either; I know that I must have had a mother, but who she was, and where she lived, by heavens, I do not know."

The colonel was silent, and seemed for a moment lost in thought. "Where did you come to know my daughter?"

"I do not know her, gracious sir; I declare I do not know her."

"Why then has she chosen you, and no one else, to offer up prayers for her?"

The philosopher shrugged his shoulders. "God only knows. It is a well-known fact that grand people often demand things which the most learned man cannot comprehend; and does not the proverb say, 'Dance, devil, as the Lord commands!'"

"Aren't you talking nonsense, Mr Philosopher?"

"May the lightning strike me on the spot if I lie."

"If she had only lived a moment longer," said the colonel sadly, "then I had certainly found out everything. She said, 'Let no one offer up prayers for me, but send, father, at once to the seminary in Kieff for the student Thomas Brutus; he shall pray three nights running for my sinful soul — he knows.' But what he really knows she never said. The poor dove could speak no more, and died. Good man, you are probably well known for your sanctity and devout life, and she has perhaps heard of you."

"What? Of me?" said the philosopher, and took a step backward in amazement. "I and sanctity!" he exclaimed, and stared at the colonel. "God help us, gracious sir! What are you saying? It was only last Holy Thursday that I paid a visit to the tart-shop."

"Well, she must at any rate have had some reason for making the arrangement, and you must begin your duties to-day."

"I should like to remark to your honour — naturally everyone who knows the Holy Scripture at all can in his measure — but I believe it would be better on this occasion to send for a deacon or subdeacon. They are learned people, and they know exactly what is to be done. I have not got a good voice, nor any official standing."

"You may say what you like, but I shall carry out all my dove's wishes. If you read the prayers for her three nights through in the proper way, I will reward you; and if not — I advise the devil himself not to oppose me!"

The colonel spoke the last words in such an emphatic way that the philosopher quite understood them.

"Follow me!" said the colonel.

They went into the hall. The colonel opened a door which was opposite his own. The philosopher remained for a few minutes in the hall in order to look about him; then he stepped over the threshold with a certain nervousness.

The whole floor of the room was covered with red cloth. In a corner under the icons of the saints, on a table covered with a gold-bordered, velvet cloth, lay the body of the girl. Tall candles, round which were wound branches of the "calina," stood at her head and feet, and burned dimly in the broad daylight. The face of the dead was not to be seen, as the inconsolable father sat before his daughter, with his back turned to the philosopher. The words which the latter overheard filled him with a certain fear.

"I do not mourn, my daughter, that in the flower of your age you have prematurely left the earth, to my grief; but I mourn, my dove, that I do not know my deadly enemy who caused your death. Had I only known that anyone could even conceive the idea of insulting you, or of speaking a disrespectful word to you, I swear by heaven he would never have seen his children again, if he had been as old as myself; nor his father and mother, if he had been young. And I would have thrown his corpse to the birds of the air, and the wild beasts of the steppe. But woe is me, my flower, my dove, my light! I will spend the remainder of my life without joy, and wipe the bitter tears which flow out of my old eyes, while my enemy will rejoice and laugh in secret over the helpless old man!"

He paused, overpowered by grief, and streams of tears flowed down his cheeks.

The philosopher was deeply affected by the sight of such inconsolable sorrow. He coughed gently in order to clear his throat. The colonel turned and signed to him to take his place at the head of the dead girl, before a little prayer-desk on which some books lay.

"I can manage to hold out for three nights," thought the philosopher; "and then the colonel will fill both my pockets with ducats."

He approached the dead girl, and after coughing once more, began to read, without paying attention to anything else, and firmly resolved not to look at her face.

Soon there was deep silence, and he saw that the colonel had left the room. Slowly he turned his head in order to look at the corpse. A violent shudder thrilled through him; before him lay a form of such beauty as is seldom seen upon earth. It seemed to him that never in a single face had so much intensity of expression and harmony of feature been united. Her brow, soft as snow and pure as silver, seemed to be thinking; the fine, regular eyebrows shadowed proudly the closed eyes, whose lashes gently rested on her cheeks, which seemed to glow with secret longing; her lips still appeared to smile. But at the same time he saw something in these features which appalled him; a terrible depression seized his heart, as when in the midst of dance and song someone begins to chant a dirge. He felt as though those ruby lips were coloured with his own heart's blood. Moreover, her face seemed dreadfully familiar.

"The witch!" he cried out in a voice which sounded strange to himself; then he turned away and began to read the prayers with white cheeks. It was the witch whom he had killed.

II

When the sun had sunk below the horizon, the corpse was carried into the church. The philosopher supported one corner of the black- draped coffin upon his shoulder, and felt an ice-cold shiver run through his body. The colonel walked in front of him, with his right hand resting on the edge of the coffin.

The wooden church, black with age and overgrown with green lichen, stood quite at the end of the village in gloomy solitude; it was adorned with three round cupolas. One saw at the first glance that it had not been used for divine worship for a long time.

Lighted candles were standing before almost every icon. The coffin was set down before the altar. The old colonel kissed his dead daughter once more, and then left the church, together with the bearers of the bier, after he had ordered his servants to look after the philosopher and to take him back to the church after supper.

The coffin-bearers, when they returned to the house, all laid their hands on the stove. This custom is always observed in Little Eussia by those who have seen a corpse.

The hunger which the philosopher now began to feel caused him for a while to forget the dead girl altogether.

Gradually all the domestics of the house assembled in the kitchen; it was really
a kind of club, where they were accustomed to gather. Even the dogs came to the door, wagging their tails in order to have bones and offal thrown to them.

If a servant was sent on an errand, he always found his way into the kitchen to rest there for a while, and to smoke a pipe. All the Cossacks of the establishment lay here during the whole day on and under the benches — in fact, wherever a place could be found to lie down in. Moreover, everyone was always leaving something behind in the kitchen — his cap, or his whip, or something of the sort. But the numbers of the club were not complete till the evening, when the groom came in after tying up his horses in the stable, the cowherd had shut up his cows in their stalls, and others collected there who were not usually seen in the day-time. During supper-time even the tongues of the laziest were set in motion. They talked of all and everything — of the new pair of breeches which some- one had ordered for himself, of what might be in the centre of the earth, and of the wolf which someone had seen. There were a number of wits in the company — a class which is always represented in Little Eussia.

The philosopher took his place with the rest in the great circle which sat round the kitchen door in the open-air. Soon an old woman with a red cap issued from it, bearing with both hands a large vessel full of hot "galuchkis," which she distributed among them. Each drew out of his pocket a wooden spoon, or a one-pronged wooden fork. As soon as their jaws began to move a little more slowly, and their wolfish hunger was somewhat appeased, they began to talk. The conversation, as might be expected, turned on the dead girl.

"Is it true" said a young shepherd, "is it true — though I cannot understand it — that our young mistress had traffic with evil spirits?"

"Who, the young lady?" answered Dorosch, whose acquaintance the philosopher had already made in the kibitka. "Yes, she was a regular witch! I can swear that she was a witch!"

"Hold your tongue, Dorosch!" exclaimed another — the one who, during the journey, had played the part of a consoler. "We have nothing to do with that. May God be merciful to her! One ought not to talk of such things."

But Dorosch was not at all inclined to be silent; he had just visited the wine-cellar with the steward on important business, and having stooped two or three times over one or two casks, he had returned in a very cheerful and loquacious mood.

"Why do you ask me to be silent?" he answered. "She has ridden on my own shoulders, I swear she has."

"Say, uncle," asked the young shepherd, "are there signs by which to recognise a sorceress?"

"No, there are not," answered Dorosch; "even if you knew the Psalter by heart, you could not recognise one."

"Yes, Dorosch, it is possible; don't talk such nonsense," retorted the former consoler. "It is not for nothing that God has given each some special peculiarity; the learned maintain that every witch has a little tail."

"Every old woman is a witch," said a grey-headed Cossack quite seriously.

"Yes, you are a fine lot," retorted the old woman who entered at that moment with a vessel full of fresh "galuchkis."[16] "You are great fat pigs!"

A self-satisfied smile played round the lips of the old Cossack whose name was Javtuch, when he found that his remark had touched the old woman on a tender point. The shepherd burst into such a deep and loud explosion of laughter as if two oxen were lowing together.

This conversation excited in the philosopher a great curiosity, and a wish to obtain more exact information regarding the colonel's daughter. In order to lead the talk back to the subject, he turned to his next neighbour and said, "I should like to know why all the people here think that the young lady was a witch. Has she done harm to anyone, or killed them by witchcraft?"

"Yes, there are reports of that kind," answered a man, whose face was as flat as a shovel. "Who does not remember the huntsman Mikita, or the–"

"What has the huntsman Mikita got to do with it?" asked the philosopher.

"Stop; I will tell you the story of Mikita," interrupted Dorosch.

"No, I will tell it," said the groom, "for he was my godfather."

"I will tell the story of Mikita," said Spirid.

---

[16] A Ukrainian dumpling cooked in broth.

"Yes, yes, Spirid shall tell it," exclaimed the whole company; and Spirid began.

"You, Mr Philosopher Thomas, did not know Mikita. Ah! he was an extraordinary man. He knew every dog as though he were his own father. The present huntsman, Mikola, who sits three places away from me, is not fit to hold a candle to him, though good enough in his way; but compared to Mikita, he is a mere milksop."

"You tell the tale splendidly," exclaimed Dorosch, and nodded as a sign of approval.

Spirid continued.

"He saw a hare in the field quicker than you can take a pinch of snuff. He only needed to whistle 'Come here, Easboy! Come here, Bosdraja!' and flew away on his horse like the wind, so that you could not say whether he went quicker than the dog or the dog than he. He could empty a quart pot of brandy in the twinkling of an eye. Ah! he was a splendid huntsman, only for some time he always had his eyes fixed on the young lady. Either he had fallen in love with her or she had bewitched him — in short, he went to the dogs. He became a regular old woman; yes, he became the devil knows what — it is not fitting to relate it."

"Very good," remarked Dorosch.

"If the young lady only looked at him, he let the reins slip out of his hands, called Bravko instead of Easboy, stumbled, and made all kinds of mistakes. One day when he was currycombing a horse, the young lady came to him in the stable. 'Listen, Mikita,' she said. 'I should like for once to set my foot on you.' And he, the booby, was quite delighted, and answered, 'Don't only set your foot there, but sit on me altogether.' The young lady lifted her white little foot, and as soon as he saw it, his delight robbed him of his senses. He bowed his neck, the idiot, took her feet in both hands, and began to trot about like a horse all over the place. Whither they went he could not say; he returned more dead than alive, and from that time he wasted away and became as dry as a chip of wood. At last someone coming into the stable one day found instead of him only a handful of ashes and an empty jug; he had burned completely out. But it must be said he was a huntsman such as the world cannot match."

When Spirid had ended his tale, they all began to vie with one another in praising the deceased huntsman.

"And have you heard the story of Cheptchicha?" asked Dorosch, turning to Thomas.

"No."

"Ha! Ha! One sees they don't teach you much in your seminary. Well, listen. We have here in our village a Cossack called Cheptoun, a fine fellow. Sometimes indeed he amuses himself by stealing and lying without any reason; but he is a fine fellow for all that. His house is not far away from here. One evening, just about this time, Cheptoun and his wife went to bed after they had finished their day's work. Since it was fine weather, Cheptchicha went to sleep in the court-yard, and Cheptoun in the house — no! I mean Cheptchicha went to sleep in the house on a bench and Cheptoun outside."

"No, Cheptchicha didn't go to sleep on a bench, but on the ground," interrupted the old woman who stood at the door.

Dorosch looked at her, then at the ground, then again at her, and said after a pause, "If I tore your dress off your back before all these people, it wouldn't look pretty."

The rebuke was effectual. The old woman was silent, and did not interrupt again.

Dorosch continued.

"In the cradle which hung in the middle of the room lay a one-year-old child. I do not know whether it was a boy or a girl. Cheptchicha had lain down, and heard on the other side of the door a dog scratching and howling loud enough to frighten anyone. She was afraid, for women are such simple folk that if one puts out one's tongue at them behind the door in the dark, their hearts sink into their boots. 'But,' she thought to herself, 'I must give this cursed dog one on the snout to stop his howling!? So she seized the poker and opened the door. But hardly had she done so than the dog rushed between her legs straight to the cradle. Then Cheptchicha saw that it was not a dog but the young lady; and if it had only been the young lady as she knew her it wouldn't have mattered, but she looked quite blue, and her eyes sparkled like fiery coals. She seized the child, bit its throat, and began to suck its blood. Cheptchicha shrieked, 'Ah! my darling child!' and rushed out of the room. Then she saw that the house-door was shut and rushed up to the attic and sat there, the stupid woman, trembling all over. Then the young lady came after her and bit her too, poor fool! The next morning Cheptoun carried his wife, all bitten and wounded, down from the attic, and the next day she died. Such strange things happen in the world. One may wear fine clothes, but that does not matter; a witch is and remains a witch.”

After telling his story, Dorosch looked around him with a complacent air, and cleaned out his pipe with his little finger in order to fill it again. The story of the witch had made a deep impression on all, and each of them had something to say about her. One had seen her come to the door of his house in the form of a hayrick; from others she had stolen their caps or their pipes; she had cut off the hair-plaits of many girls in the village, and drunk whole pints of the blood of others.

At last the whole company observed that they had gossiped over their time, for it was already night. All looked for a sleeping place — some in the kitchen and others in the barn or the courtyard.

“Now, Mr Thomas, it is time that we go to the dead,” said the grey-headed Cossack, turning to the philosopher. All four — Spirid, Dorosch, the old Cossack, and the philosopher — betook themselves to the church, keeping off with their whips the wild dogs who roamed about the roads in great numbers and bit the sticks of passers-by in sheer malice.

Although the philosopher had seized the opportunity of fortifying himself beforehand with a stiff glass of brandy, yet he felt a certain secret fear which increased as he approached the church, which was lit up within. The strange tales he had heard had made a deep impression on his imagination. They had passed the thick hedges and trees, and the country became more open. At last they reached the small enclosure round the church; behind it there were no more trees, but a huge, empty plain dimly visible in the darkness. The three Cossacks ascended the steep steps with Thomas, and entered the church. Here they left the philosopher, expressing their hope that he would successfully accomplish his duties, and locked him in as their master had ordered.

He was left alone. At first he yawned, then he stretched himself, blew on both hands, and finally looked round him. In the middle of the church stood the black bier; before the dark pictures of saints burned the candles, whose light only illuminated the icons, and cast a faint glimmer into the body of the church; all the corners were in complete darkness. The lofty icons seemed to be of considerable age; only a little of the original gilt remained on their broken traceries; the faces of the saints had become quite black and looked uncanny.

Once more the philosopher cast a glance around him. "Bother it!" said he to himself. "What is there to be afraid about? No living creature can get in, and as for the dead and those who come from the 'other side.' I can protect myself with such effectual prayers that they cannot touch me with the tips of their fingers. There is nothing to fear," he repeated, swinging his arms. "Let us begin the prayers!"

As he approached one of the side-aisles, he noticed two packets of candles which had been placed there.

"That is fine," he thought. "I must illuminate the whole church, till it is as bright as day. What a pity that one cannot smoke in it."

He began to light the candles on all the wall-brackets and all the candelabra, as well as those already burning before the holy pictures; soon the whole church was brilliantly lit up. Only the darkness in the roof above seemed still denser by contrast, and the faces of the saints peering out of the frames looked as unearthly as before. He approached the bier, looked nervously at the face of the dead girl, could not help shuddering slightly, and involuntarily closed his eyes. What terrible and extraordinary beauty!

He turned away and tried to go to one side, but the strange curiosity and peculiar fascination which men feel in moments of fear, compelled him to look again and again, though with a similar shudder. And in truth there was something terrible about the beauty of the dead girl. Perhaps she would not have inspired so much fear had she been less beautiful; but there was nothing ghastly or deathlike in the face, which wore rather an expression of life, and it seemed to the philosopher as though she were watching him from under her closed eyelids. He even thought he saw a tear roll from under the eye- lash of her right eye, but when it was half-way down her cheek, he saw that it was a drop of blood.

He quickly went into one of the stalls, opened his book, and began to read the prayers in a very loud voice in order to keep up his courage. His deep voice sounded strange to himself in the grave-like silence; it aroused no echo in the silent and desolate wooden walls of the church.

"What is there to be afraid of?" he thought to himself. "She will not rise from her bier, since she fears God's word. She will remain quietly resting. Yes, and what sort of a

Cossack should I be, if I were afraid? The fact is, I have drunk a little too much — that is why I feel so queer. Let me take a pinch of snuff. It is really excellent — first-rate!"

At the same time he cast a furtive glance over the pages of the prayer-book towards the bier, and involuntarily he said to himself, "There! See! She is getting up! Her head is already above the edge of the coffin!"

But a death-like silence prevailed; the coffin was motionless, and all the candles shone steadily. It was an awe-inspiring sight, this church lit up at midnight, with the corpse in the midst, and no living soul near but one. The philosopher began to sing in various keys in order to stifle his fears, but every moment he glanced across at the coffin, and involuntarily the question came to his lips, "Suppose she rose up after all?"

But the coffin did not move. Nowhere was there the slightest sound nor stir. Not even did a cricket chirp in any corner. There was nothing audible but the slight sputtering of some distant candle, or the faint fall of a drop of wax.

"Suppose she rose up after all?"

He raised his head. Then he looked round him wildly and rubbed his eyes. Yes, she was no longer lying in the coffin, but sitting upright. He turned away his eyes, but at once looked again, terrified, at the coffin. She stood up; then she walked with closed eyes through the church, stretching out her arms as though she wanted to seize someone.

She now came straight towards him. Full of alarm, he traced with his finger a circle round himself; then in a loud voice he began to recite the prayers and formulas of exorcism which he had learnt from a monk who had often seen witches and evil spirits.

She had almost reached the edge of the circle which he had traced; but it was evident that she had not the power to enter it. Her face wore a bluish tint like that of one who has been several days dead.

Thomas had not the courage to look at her, so terrible was her appearance; her teeth chattered and she opened her dead eyes, but as in her rage she saw nothing, she turned in another direction and felt with outstretched arms among the pillars and corners of the church in the hope of seizing him.

At last she stood still, made a threatening gesture, and then lay down again in the coffin.

The philosopher could not recover his self-possession, and kept on gazing anxiously at it. Suddenly it rose from its place and began hurtling about the church with a whizzing sound. At one time it was almost directly over his head; but the philosopher observed that it could not pass over the area of his charmed circle, so he kept on repeating his formulas of exorcism. The coffin now fell with a crash in the middle of the church, and remained lying there motionless. The corpse rose again; it had now a greenish-blue colour, but at the same moment the distant crowing of a cock was audible, and it lay down again.

The philosopher's heart beat violently, and the perspiration poured in streams from his face; but heartened by the crowing of the cock, he rapidly repeated the prayers.

As the first light of dawn looked through the windows, there came a deacon and the grey-haired Javtuk, who acted as sacristan, in order to release him. When he had reached the house, he could not sleep for a long time; but at last weariness overpowered him, and he slept till noon. When he awoke, his experiences of the night appeared to him like a dream. He was given a quart of brandy to strengthen him.

At table he was again talkative and ate a fairly large sucking pig almost without assistance. But none the less he resolved to say nothing of what he had seen, and to all curious questions only returned the answer, "Yes, some wonderful things happened."

The philosopher was one of those men who, when they have had a good meal, are uncommonly amiable. He lay down on a bench, with his pipe in his mouth, looked blandly at all, and expectorated every minute.

But as the evening approached, he became more and more pensive. About supper-time nearly the whole company had assembled in order to play "krapli." This is a kind of game of skittles, in which, instead of bowls, long staves are used, and the winner has the right to ride on the back of his opponent. It provided the spectators with much amusement; sometimes the groom, a huge man, would clamber on the back of the swineherd, who was slim and short and shrunken; another time the groom would present his own back, while Dorosch sprang on it shouting, "What a regular ox!" Those of the company who were more staid sat by the threshold of the kitchen. They looked uncommonly serious, smoked their pipes, and did not even smile when the younger ones went into fits of laughter over some joke of the groom or Spirid.

Thomas vainly attempted to take part in the game; a gloomy thought was firmly fixed like a nail in his head. In spite of his desperate efforts to appear cheerful after supper, fear had over- mastered his whole being, and it increased with the growing darkness.

"Now it is time for us to go, Mr Student!" said the grey-haired Cossack, and stood up with Dorosch. "Let us betake ourselves to our work."

Thomas was conducted to the church in the same way as on the previous evening; again he was left alone, and the door was bolted behind him.

As soon as he found himself alone, he began to feel in the grip of his fears. He again saw the dark pictures of the saints in their gilt frames, and the black coffin, which stood menacing and silent in the middle of the church.

"Never mind!" he said to himself. "I am over the first shock. The first time I was frightened, but I am not so at all now — no, not at all!"

He quickly went into a stall, drew a circle round him with his finger, uttered some prayers and formulas for exorcism, and then began to read the prayers for the dead in a loud voice and with the fixed resolution not to look up from the book nor take notice of anything.

He did so for an hour, and began to grow a little tired; he cleared his throat and drew his snuff-box out of his pocket, but before he had taken a pinch he looked nervously towards the coffin.

A sudden chill shot through him. The witch was already standing before him on the edge of the circle, and had fastened her green eyes upon him. He shuddered, looked down at the book, and began to read his prayers and exorcisms aloud. Yet all the while he was aware how her teeth chattered, and how she stretched out her arms to seize him. But when he cast a hasty glance towards her, he saw that she was not looking in his direction, and it was clear that she could not see him.

Then she began to murmur in an undertone, and terrible words escaped her lips — words that sounded like the bubbling of boiling pitch. The philosopher did not know their meaning, but he knew that they signified something terrible, and were intended to counteract his exorcisms.

After she had spoken, a stormy wind arose in the church, and there was a noise like the rushing of many birds. He heard the noise of their wings and claws as they flapped against and scratched at the iron bars of the church windows. There were also violent blows on the church door, as if someone were trying to break it in pieces.

The philosopher's heart beat violently; he did not dare to look up, but continued to read the prayers without a pause. At last there was heard in the distance the shrill sound of a cock's crow. The exhausted philosopher stopped and gave a great sigh of relief.

Those who came to release him found him more dead than alive; he had leant his back against the wall, and stood motionless, regarding them without any expression in his eyes. They were obliged almost to carry him to the house; he then shook himself, asked for and drank a quart of brandy. He passed his hand through his hair and said, "There are all sorts of horrors in the world, and such dreadful things happen that–" Here he made a gesture as though to ward off something. All who heard him bent their heads forward in curiosity. Even a small boy, who ran on everyone's errands, stood by with his mouth wide open.

Just then a young woman in a close-fitting dress passed by. She was the old cook's assistant, and very coquettish; she always stuck something in her bodice by way of ornament, a ribbon or a flower, or even a piece of paper if she could find nothing else.

"Good day, Thomas," she said, as she saw the philosopher. "Dear me! what has happened to you?" she exclaimed, striking her hands together.

"Well, what is it, you silly creature?"

"Good heavens! You have grown quite grey!"

"Yes, so he has!" said Spirid, regarding him more closely. " You have grown as grey as our old Javtuk."

When the philosopher heard that, he hastened into the kitchen, where he had noticed on the wall a dirty, three-cornered piece of looking-glass. In front of it hung some forget-me-nots, evergreens, and a small garland — a proof that it was the toilette-glass of the young coquette. With alarm he saw that it actually was as they had said — his hair was quite grizzled.

He sank into a reverie; at last he said to himself, "I will go to the colonel, tell him all, and declare that I will read no more prayers. He must send me back at once to Kieff." With this intention he turned towards the door-steps of the colonel's house.

The colonel was sitting motionless in his room; his face displayed the same hopeless grief which Thomas had observed on it on his first arrival, only the hollows in his cheeks had deepened. It was obvious that he took very little or no food. A strange paleness made him look almost aa though made of marble.

"Good day," he said as he observed Thomas standing, cap in hand, at the door. "Well, how are you getting on? All right?"

"Yes, sir, all right! Such hellish things are going on, that one would like to rush away as far as one's feet can carry one."

"How so?"

"Your daughter, sir. When one considers the matter, she is, of course, of noble descent — no one can dispute that; but don't be angry, and may God grant her eternal rest!"

"Very well! What about her?"

"She is in league with the devil. She inspires one with such dread that all prayers are useless."

"Pray! Pray! It was not for nothing that she sent for you. My dove was troubled about her salvation, and wished to expel all evil influences by means of prayer."

"I swear, gracious sir, it is beyond my power."

"Pray! Pray!" continued the colonel in the same persuasive tone. "There is only one night more; you are doing a Christian work, and I will reward you richly."

"However great your rewards may be, I will not read the prayers any more, sir," said Thomas in a tone of decision.

"Listen, philosopher!" said the colonel with a menacing air. "I will not allow any objections. In your seminary you may act as you like, but here it won't do. If I have you knouted,[17] it will be somewhat different to the rector's canings.[18] Do you know what a strong 'kantchuk'[19] is?"

"Of course I do," said the philosopher in a low voice; "a number of them together are insupportable."

"Yes, I think so too. But you don't know yet how hot my fellows can make it," replied the colonel threateningly. He sprang up, and his face assumed a fierce, despotic expression, betraying the savagery of his nature, which had been only temporarily modified by grief. "Small scourge." After the first flogging they pour on brandy and then repeat it. Go away and finish your work. If you don't obey, you

---

[17] Whip having multiple rawhide tendrils.

[18] Struck with a cane.

[19] A short-handled whip.

won't be able to stand again, and if you do, you will get a thousand ducats."[20]

"That is a devil of a fellow," thought the philosopher to himself, and went out. "One can't trifle with him. But wait a little, my friend; I will escape you so cleverly, that even your hounds can't find me!"

He determined, under any circumstances, to run away, and only waited till the hour after dinner arrived, when all the servants were accustomed to take a nap on the hay in the barn, and to snore and puff so loudly that it sounded as if machinery had been set up there. At last the time came. Even Javtuch stretched himself out in the sun and closed his eyes. Tremblingly, and on tiptoe, the philosopher stole softly into the garden, whence he thought he could escape more easily into the open country. This garden was generally so choked up with weeds that it seemed admirably adapted for such an attempt. With the exception of a single path used by the people of the house, the whole of it was covered with cherry-trees, elder-bushes, and tall heath-thistles with fibrous red buds. All these trees and bushes had been thickly overgrown with ivy, which formed a kind of roof. Its tendrils reached to the hedge and fell down on the other side in snake-like curves among the small, wild field-flowers. Behind the hedge which bordered the garden was a dense mass of wild heather, in which it did not seem probable that anyone would care to venture himself, and the strong, stubborn stems of which seemed likely to baffle any attempt to cut them.

As the philosopher was about to climb over the hedge, his teeth chattered, and his heart beat s0 violently that he felt frightened at it. The skirts of his long cloak seemed to cling to the ground as though they had been fastened to it by pegs. When he had actually got over the hedge he seemed to hear a shrill voice crying behind him "Whither? Whither?"

He jumped into the heather and began to run, stumbling over old roots and treading on unfortunate moles. When He had emerged from the heather he saw that he still had a wide field to cross, behind which was a thick, thorny under-wood. This, according to his calculation, must stretch as far as the road leading to Kieff, and if he reached it he would be safe. Accordingly He ran over the

---

[20] A currency coin, many times a gold coin.

field and plunged into the thorny copse. Every sharp thorn he encountered tore a fragment from His coat. Then He reached a small open space; in the centre of it stood a willow, whose branches hung down to the earth, and close by flowed a clear spring bright as silver. The first thing the philosopher did was to lie down and drink eagerly, for he was intolerably thirsty.

"Splendid water!" he said, wiping his mouth. "This is a good place to rest in."

"No, better run farther; perhaps we are being followed," said a voice immediately behind him.

Thomas started and turned; before him stood Javtuch.

"This devil of a Javtuch!" he thought. "I should like to seize him by the feet and smash his hang-dog face against the trunk of a tree."

"Why did you go round such a long way?" continued Javtuch. "You had much better have chosen the path by which I came; it leads directly by the stable. Besides, it is a pity about your coat. Such splendid cloth! How much did it cost an ell? Well, we have had a long enough walk; it is time to go home."

The philosopher followed Javtuch in a very depressed state.

"Now the accursed witch will attack me in earnest," he thought. "But what have I really to fear? Am I not a Cossack? I have read the prayers for two nights already; with God's help I will get through the third night also. It is plain that the witch must have a terrible load of guilt upon her, else the evil one would not help her so much."

Feeling somewhat encouraged by these reflections, he returned to the court-yard and asked D'orosch, who sometimes, by the steward's permission, had access to the wine-cellar, to fetch him a small bottle of brandy. The two friends sat down before a barn and drank a pretty large one. Suddenly the philosopher jumped up and said, "I want musicians! Bring some musicians!"

But without waiting for them he began to dance the "tropak" in the court-yard. He danced till tea-time, and the servants, who, as is usual in such cases, had formed a small circle round him, grew at last tired of watching him, and went away saying, "By heavens, the man can dance!"

Finally the philosopher lay down in the place where he had been dancing, and fell asleep. It was necessary to pour a bucket of cold water on his head to wake him up for supper. At the meal he enlarged on the topic of what a

Cossack ought to be, and how he should not be afraid of anything in the world.

"It is time," said Javtuch; "let us go."

"I wish I could put a lighted match to your tongue," thought the philosopher; then he stood up and said, "let us go."

On their way to the church, the philosopher kept looking round him on all sides, and tried to start a conversation with his companions; but both Javtuch and Dorosch remained silent. It was a weird night. In the distance wolves howled continually, and even the barking of the dogs had something unearthly about it.

"That doesn't sound like wolves howling, but something else," remarked Dorosch.

Javtuch still kept silent, and the philosopher did not know what answer to make.

They reached the church and walked over the old wooden planks, whose rotten condition showed how little the lord of the manor cared about God and his soul. Javtuch and Dorosch left the philosopher alone, as on the previous evenings.

There was still the same atmosphere of menacing silence in the church, in the centre of which stood the coffin with the terrible witch inside it.

"I am not afraid, by heavens, I am not afraid!" he said; and after drawing a circle round himself as before, he began to read the prayers and exorcisms.

An oppressive silence prevailed; the flickering candles filled the church with their clear light. The philosopher turned one page after another, and noticed that he was not reading what was in the book. Full of alarm, he crossed himself and began to sing a hymn. This calmed him somewhat, and he resumed his reading, turning the pages rapidly as he did so.

Suddenly in the midst of the sepulchral silence the iron lid of the coffin sprang open with a jarring noise, and the dead witch stood up. She was this time still more terrible in aspect than at

first. Her teeth chattered loudly and her lips, through which poured a stream of dreadful curses, moved convulsively. A whirlwind arose in the church; the icons of the saints fell on the ground, together with the broken window-panes. The door was wrenched from its hinges, and a huge mass of monstrous creatures rushed into the church, which became filled with the noise of beating wings and scratching claws. All these creatures flew and crept about, seeking for the philosopher, from whose brain the last fumes of intoxication had vanished. He crossed himself ceaselessly and uttered prayer after prayer, hearing all the time the whole unclean swarm rustling about him, and brushing him with the tips of their wings. He had not the courage to look at them; he only saw one uncouth monster standing by the wall, with long, shaggy hair and two flaming eyes. Over him something hung in the air which looked like a gigantic bladder covered with countless crabs' claws and scorpions' stings, and with black clods of earth hanging from it. All these monsters stared about seeking him, but they could not find him, since he was protected by his sacred circle.

"Bring the Viy! Bring the Viy!" cried the witch.

A sudden silence followed; the howling of wolves was heard in the distance, and soon heavy footsteps resounded through the church. Thomas looked up furtively and saw that an ungainly human figure with crooked legs was being led into the church. He was quite covered with black soil, and his hands and feet resembled knotted roots. He trod heavily and stumbled at every step. His eyelids were of enormous length. With terror, Thomas saw that his face was of iron. They led him in by the arms and placed him near Thomas's circle.

"Raise my eyelids! I can't see anything!" said the Viy in a dull, hollow voice, and they all hastened to help in doing so.

"Don't look!" an inner voice warned the philosopher; but he could not restrain from looking.

"There he is!" exclaimed the Viy, pointing an iron finger at him, and all the monsters rushed on him at once.

Struck dumb with terror, he sank to the ground and died.

At that moment there sounded a cock's crow for the second time; the earth-spirits had not heard the first one. In alarm they hurried to the windows and the door to get out as quickly as possible. But it was too late; they all remained hanging as though fastened to the door and the windows.

When the priest came he stood amazed at such a desecration of God's house, and did not venture to read prayers there. The church remained standing as it was, with the monsters hanging on the windows and the door.

Gradually it became overgrown with creepers, bushes, and wild heather, and no one can discover it now.

When the report of this event reached Kieff, and the theologian Khalava heard what a fate had overtaken the philosopher Thomas, he sank for a whole hour into deep reflection. He had greatly altered of late; after finishing his studies he had become bell-ringer of one of the chief churches in the city, and he always appeared with a bruised nose, because the belfry staircase was in a ruinous condition.

"Have you heard what has happened to Thomas?" said Tiberius Gorobetz, who had become a philosopher and now wore a moustache.

"Yes; God had appointed it so," answered the bell-ringer. "Let us go to the ale-house; we will drink a glass to his memory."

The young philosopher, who, with the enthusiasm of a novice, had made such full use of his privileges as a student that his breeches and coat and even his cap reeked of brandy and tobacco, agreed readily to the proposal.

"He was a fine fellow, Thomas," said the bell-ringer as the limping innkeeper set the third jug of beer before him. "A splendid fellow! And lost his life for nothing!"

"I know why he perished," said Gorobetz; "because he was afraid. If he had not feared her, the witch could have done nothing to him. One ought to cross oneself incessantly and spit exactly on her tail, and then not the least harm can happen. I know all about it, for here, in Kieff, all the old women in the market-place are witches."

The bell-ringer nodded assent. But being aware that he could not say any more, he got up cautiously and went out, swaying to the right and left in order to find a hiding-place in the thick steppe grass outside the town. At the same time, in accordance with his old habits, he did not forget to steal an old boot-sole which lay on the ale-house bench.

*****

Witch Short Stories Considered

<u>Anonymous</u>
(1800-1820) The Lunatic and His Turkey
1825 The Irish Witch and the Rebel's Wife
1827 The Yarmouth Witch
1828 The Hot-Tongs Society. An Angler's Adventure
1835 The Witch
1835 The Witch of Rosberry Topping, or the Haunted Ring
1839 The Witch Spectre
1847 The Magic Draught. A Tale of the Restoration.

<u>William Darby "Mark Bancroft"</u>
1836 Lydia Ashbaugh, The Witch

<u>Alexander Dumas</u>
1840s The Enchanted Whistle

<u>Nikolai Gogol</u>
1835 Viy

<u>William Child Green</u>
1842 Secrets of Cabalism, or Ravenstone and Alice of
Huntington

<u>Wilhelm Hauff</u>
1827 Nosey, the Dwarf
1827 The Prophecy of the Silver Florin

<u>Nathaniel Hawthorne</u>
1830 The Hollow of the Three Hills
1835 Young Goodman Brown

<u>James Hogg</u>
1818 The Hunt of Eildon
1827 The Brownie of the Black Haggs
1829 A Strange Secret
1837 The Witches of Traquair

<u>Thomas Ingoldsby</u>
1840 Mrs. Brotherby's Story: The Leech of Folkestone

<u>Samuel Lover "Handy Andy"</u>

1847 The Marvelous Legend of Tom Connor's Cat

<u>James Kirke Paulding</u>
1838 The Nameless Old Woman

<u>Charles Pigault-Lebrun (1753-1835)</u>
1825 The Unholy Compact Abjured; or, The Heroism of Love

<u>Alicia S.</u>
1843 The Witch of the Glen

<u>Ludwig Tieck</u>
1823 The Sorcerers

About Andrew Barger

Andrew is the author of *The Divine Dantes* trilogy and *Coffee with Poe: A Novel of Edgar Allan Poe's Life*. He has edited a number of highly regarded anthologies, focusing on the best short stories of the 19th century. Andrew's first short story collection is *Mailboxes – Mansions – Memphistopheles*.

He is recognized for his scholarly and creative writing and is a leading voice in the Gothic literature space. His most recent scholarly Poe article was published by Johns Hopkins Press: Andrew Barger, "Frances Osgood's Connections to Edgar Allan Poe's Couplet and the Stuart Manuscript of 'Eulalie,'" *Poe Studies*, 55 (2022): 109-25.

Andrew would like to start a band if only he could settle on a name for it.

Connect with Andrew Online

Website: AndrewBarger.com
Blog: AndrewBarger.blogspot.com
Facebook.com/AuthorAndrewBarger
goodreads.com/author/show/1362598.Andrew_Barger

Read Other Titles by Andrew Barger

Fiction

Coffee with Poe: A Novel of Edgar Allan Poe's Life
The Divine Dantes: Squirt Guns in Hades (Book I)
The Divine Dantes: Paella in Purgatory (Book II)
The Divine Dantes: Cruising in Paradise (Book III)
Mailboxes – Mansions – Memphistopheles

Anthologies Edited

1800-1849

Shifters: Best Werewolf Short Stories 1800-1849
Middle Unearthed: Best Fantasy Short Stories 1800-1849
BlooDeath: Best Vampire Stories 1800-1849
Mesaerion: Best Science Fiction Stories 1800-1849
Phantasmal: Best Ghost Stories 1800-1849
6a66le: Best Horror Short Stories 1800-1849
Orion: An Epic English Poem

1850-1899

Fright: Best Horror Short Stories 1850-1899
Specters: Best Ghost Short Stories 1850-1899
Leo Tolstoy's 20 Greatest Short Stories Annotated
Leo Tolstoy's 5 Greatest Novellas Annotated

Intellectual Property

© Copyright Bottletree Books LLC All rights reserved. ISBN: 978-1-933747-68-2. Andrew Barger is part owner of Bottletree Books LLC. Digital images of the cover may be resized and shown as "fair use" for purposes of selling and promoting the book. This work and all names, characters, places and incidents are fictional. Any resemblance to actual events or locals or persons, living or dead, is coincidental. BOTTLETREE, the Bottletree logo, and related trade dress, including all cover art designs are trademarks of Bottletree Books, LLC.

www.ingramcontent.com/pod-product-compliance
Lightning Source LLC
Chambersburg PA
CBHW030804190726
48285CB00003B/1021